MONDAY

September 8, 2025

CHAPTER 1

Max stood on the Main Street sidewalk out front of Mister Quickie's copy shop, waiting to be taken for a ride by Clark "Dumbo" Dumphy. That was how wheeler-dealers rolled, always on the move to the next big deal, never letting the grass grow under their…wheels.

Dumphy had already made a bundle in various ventures and now, thanks to their moms being members of the same yoga class, Yours Truly was in line to come up with a golden goose egg. All he had to do to get into the high-roller derby was…

Honk. Honk. Honk.

What in Sam Hill? A little orange car came wrong-way down a lane of Main Street, and at the wheel…

Honk. Honk. Honk.

…Dumbo made a spinning motion with the finger of a raised hand that must have been intended to signal his intention to skate around the block and get into the right lane for the scheduled pick up.

Max sighed.

Despite his handle, Dumbo was physically a small fry, naturally able to get into and out of tight spaces such as front seats of compact cars. Yours Truly, on the other hand, had been naturally born pear-shaped and heavyset. After growing up and walking a mail route for twelve-plus years, followed by another twelve-plus years of service in the post office sorting room, he had become even heavierset. In retirement—with nothing to do except re-read private dick case reports from back in the *Noir*, re-watch documentaries of cases worked by famous gumshoes, and snack—he would have ballooned to three-hundred pounds if not for…

Praise the Lord, while Googling for a fat man help site, he had discovered that back in the mid-1940s a jotter named Dashiell Hammett, case reporter for Sam Spade and Nick Charles a/k/a "The Thin Man", had also written up for radio the exploits of a third P.I. And thank God, a few episodes of the oldtime series were available on cds. Each began with the sound of heavy footsteps, followed by a woman's sultry voice:

*There he goes…into that drugstore…*sound of a coin dropping into a slot, followed by sound of a card being ejected like a dollar bill from an ATM…*Weight: two-hundred forty-three pounds… Fortune: Dangerrr…Whooo is it?*

The Fat Mannn said a voice from back in the days of *Noir*, in a baritone drawl belonging to a Brad Runyon. At long last, a heavyweight hero he could identify with.

In a matter of weeks, he had completed fifty hours of vo-tech classwork and applied for an Unarmed P.I. License. He had outfitted himself in a vintage double-breasted suit, two-tone brown-and-white shoes and felt fedora like worn by Runyon in a photo included with the cd set. He bought a shoulder-holstered plastic replica of a .45 caliber semi-automatic gat. He got Mister Quickie to let him set up shop in a workstation cubicle in return for providing Notary Public services for copy shop customers. He adopted the catchy moniker, "Maximo", and…

As Dumbo Dumphy's little MINI Cooper car came around the corner at Tenth Street, Max again sighed. No way would he be able to get into the toy vehicle to roll with…

Uh oh, a big red so-called muscle car pulled out of a parking spot, forcing Dumbo's unmuscular orange ride into the center lane. Dumbo got past the speeding red car, swerved into the right-hand lane and…Uh oh, as the high-roller came to a sudden stop for the scheduled pick-up…

BANG!

…the big red muscle car crashed into the unprotected rear end of Dumbo's much smaller wheels. Immediately…

WHEELER DEALER

A Maximo Morgan Mystery

SEPTEMBER

WILLIAM LEROY

All rights reserved. Published by Mossik Press.

mossikpress@mail.com

Library of Congress Cataloguing-in-Publication Data

LeRoy, William [10.7.2025]

Wheeler Dealer / Generation Gaps
by William LeRoy.

p. cm
ISBN 979-8-9992429-2-1

1. Humor—Fiction.
2. Oklahoma, United States—Fiction.
3. Mystery—Fiction.
4. Noir—Fiction.
I. Title

10 9 8 7 6 5 4 3 2 1

Manufactured in the United States of America
First Edition

WHEELER DEALER

SEPTEMBER

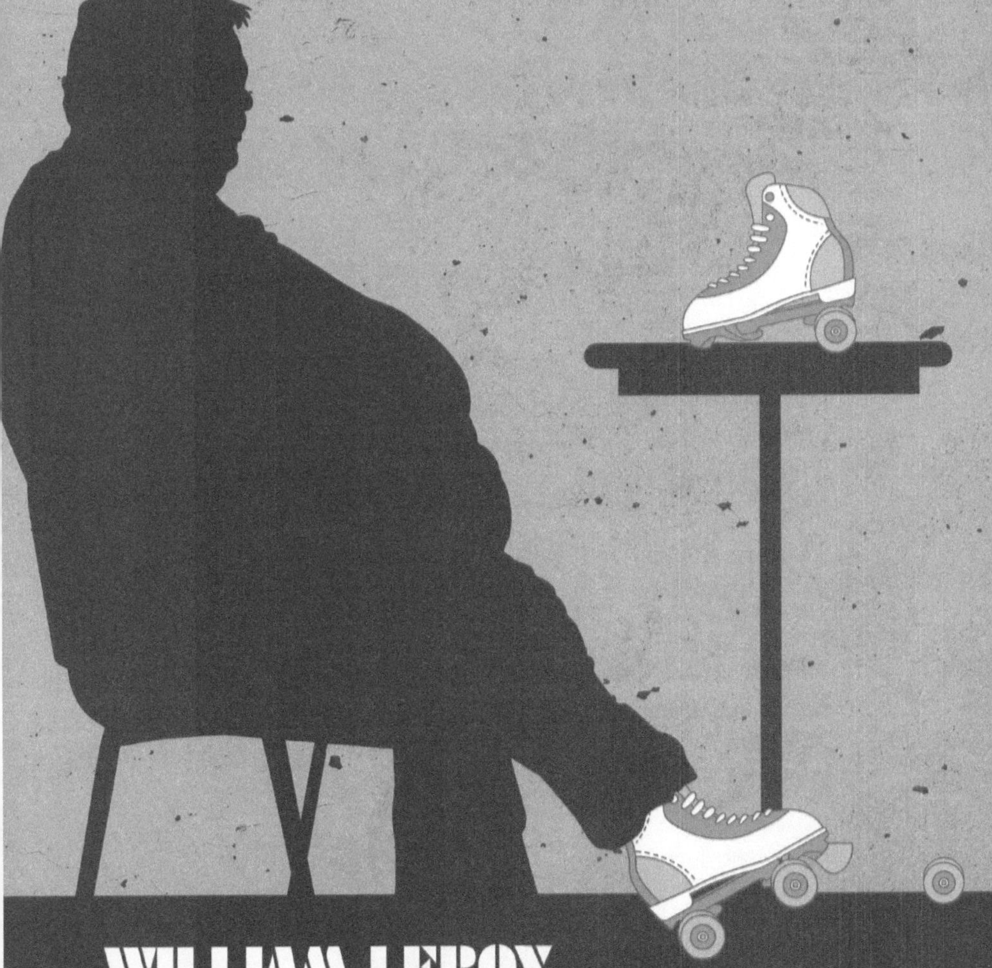

WILLIAM LEROY

EeeoooeeeOOOEEEOOO…

…a police car came racing up Main Street with its siren blaring, but…

EEEOOOEEEoooeeeooo…

…sped past the scene of the accident with its red-and-blue lights flashing.

"Did you see that, Morgan?" said Dumphy after getting out of his bent-up vehicle. "That…That pricey Rolls-Royce failed to follow at a safe distance as required by law and…Just look at the damage to the rear end of…Owww," he wailed, putting a hand to the back of his neck. "I have been whiplashed."

"No *problemo*," said Max, grabbing the wheeler-dealer by an elbow. "We can step inside my roomy copy shop cubicle to go over the details of your current big deal. My savings account checkbook is in a desk drawer, ready to rock-and-roll."

CHAPTER 2

Rhonda Dumphy *nee* Pickens gave up running traps—a/k/a searching for value in stuff put out at curbs for free monthly take away—and headed for her Easy Pickens What-n-Whatnot Shop, a secondhand goods outlet located in the former U.S. Postal Service depot on the east side of town. Since a pre-Christmas clearance sale of sorts, the store had been understocked, customer traffic was down, profits negligible. And her husband, Dumbo, was unlikely to reel in another white whale.

Last year he had conned one of his stock brokerage clients into financing purchase of the Christian Brothers Cleaners in Tulsa. His stake in the venture was encumbered with loans made by the investor but—though Dumbo was clueless about how to run any kind of business—through the years the longtime family-owned chain of six outlets had amassed a sizable stash of "off the books" assets.

Based on the company logo, a Christian cross, and advertising slogan—"Cleanliness is next to Godliness"—Dumbo had doped out that the owners were devoutly religious so-called "holy rollers". With a little digging at church functions, he discovered that their belief in the Resurrection of Jesus—as reputedly depicted by the Apostle John—was based not on John's discovery of the empty tomb *per se*, but on seeing that the linens in which Jesus' dead body had been wrapped were abandoned inside the tomb, unstained by blood, undamaged by knife or scissors, and neatly stacked, which would have been impossible except by divine intervention.

In weird observance of that belief, the owners had for decades maintained a warehouse full of customers' unclaimed items, including not only designer apparel, fur coats, even wedding dresses, but also upholstered furniture and whatnot, abandoned due to simple forgetfulness, moves to other towns, weight gains, lack of money, bad memories and…

Oh, for crying out loud, already arrived at the door of her shop was a fellow scavenger, Garrett "The Ferret" Rutledge, no doubt also having a frustrating morning and in need of a "fix" of sorts.

Rhonda got out of her pickup.

"Mornin', Easy," said Garrett, addressing her by her high school nickname "Any luck today?"

"Not much, Ferret," she answered, as always. "Some days there just ain't no fish."

"Any chance of me gettin' a sneak peek at your 'Back Alley' goods?"

"You won't find anything worth rummaging for, but have at it," she said, unlocking the door. And, alas, that was true.

As a matter of law, dry cleaning operators were required to hold customers' unclaimed articles for only thirty days, after which time they were free to dispose of them as they pleased. Donations to charities were the usual method for dumping the left-overs, but in Dumbo's hands, well, her ne'er-do-well husband got the investor to actually pay to get out of a warehouse lease, then—with his backer's not fully informed permission—slyly "donated" the stored goods to the Easy Pickens What-n-Whatnot Shop.

Together they had started selling the loot piece-by-piece, literally out of the back of a truck parked in a back alley during once-a-week barely legal "Black Market Bargain Nights".

Dumbo screwed it up of course, by jacking up prices. But one night during his absence the religiously kooky former owners of the cleaners chain showed up and—horrified to find women in the alley, "casting lots like Roman soldiers"—paid a premium to redeem all the forfeited merchandise neatly stacked in abandoned depot space. Since then, however, neither she nor

Dumbo had scored a decent-size fish, and likely never would.

For all his boasting about someday pulling off a long con, her husband was too dumb and too lazy to come up with an enticing story consisting of more than a few simple chapters. His imagination was limited to, say, reversing the mailing and return addresses, then leaving stamps off envelopes. Yes, the correspondence usually got "returned" to his targeted recipients for lack of postage, but…

Eeeoooeeeoooeeeooo…

Rhonda went outside, where a familiar white Honda van with a red bubble-light on top had pulled up to the curb. A sign propped in its windshield identified the driver as THE LONE LAWYER. A window rolled down and Clarise Kilpatrick, a fiery redheaded friend since high school, said, "Get in the van but don't buckle up!"

After attending college and law school. then working for a firm in Oklahoma City for a few years, Clarise had returned to town six months ago and, inspired by a movie titled *The Lincoln Lawyer*, had set up shop on wheels. She could not yet afford tv commercials to lure clients into "a cobwebbed parlor," she said.

iiiiiIIIIIiiiii…Base to Alpha Dog. Naked female at Walmart. 10-0…iiiiiIIIIIiiiii…

"I heard a police radio call this morning—a 10-50PI—cop code for a vehicular accident involving personal injury," Clarise reported. "When I got to the Main Street scene, guess what? Dumbo had been rear-ended and taken into a nearby copy shop. A medical crew had rolled him out and took him to a clinic before I got a chance to set a hook, but…"

iiiiiIIIIIiiiii…Alpha Dog to base. Riot in progress at Walmart. Back-up needed ASAP…iiiiiIIIIIiiiii…

"No loss, Clarise. To my knowledge, Dumbo has previously worked the swoop-and-squat con only out of town, but cops and insurance companies are sure to see through the 'Dumphy Flop'. You didn't miss out on a score."

iiiiiIIIIIiiiii…10-24! Repeat, 10-24! ASAP!

"Maybe, maybe not. Witnesses said the other car looked

expensive and that the driver was an old woman who looked to be rich. I'm on my way to Okmulgee to stake out Vultures Row—the law offices across from the County Courthouse—and hopefully snatch the roadkill before Dumbo falls into the clutches of another attorney."

iiiiiIIIIIiiiii Base to Aplha Dog. 10-18. Report in. Over.... iiiiiIIIIIiiiii…

"The reason I came by, Easy, is to advise that this would be an opportune time for you to file for divorce, to make sure you get half of any pay-off for Dumbo's personal injury before he squanders both his and your share of the marital asset."

iiiiiIIIIIiiiii…Alpha Dog to Base. Code 7. Coffee break at Arby's… iiiiiIIIIIiiiii…

Clarise had been advising her for weeks to dump Dumbo, and Rhonda had to admit that maybe she should have filed for divorce months earlier, when her no-account spouse husband made the big score in the Christian Brothers Cleaners scam. But now she was reluctant to make the move. Not because she had any interest in carrying on as Mrs. Clark Dumphy; their marital bliss had cicled down the drain years ago. But if she took legal action now…

iiiiiIIIIIiiiii… Foxtrot Unit to Base. 10-50 at intersection of South 8th and Chickasaw…iiiiiIIIIIiiiii…

"Think about it," Clarise again advised, "but without delay. Don't stay too long at the party and wake up with a morning-after headache."

iiiiiIIIIIiiiii…Foxtrot to Base. 10-50 is 10-50PI! Condition of victim is 10-45b…iiiiiIIIIIiiiii…10-52! Ambulance needed ASAP . .. iiiiiIIIIIiiiii…

"Gotta go, Easy!" said the lone lawyer-on-wheels, pushing a red dashboard button. "Hi-yo, Silver!"

Eeeoooeeeoooeeeoooeeeo…

Back inside her shop, Rhonda saw that Garrett Rutledge had ferreted a cardboard box of whatnot from a nook or cranny, and was now standing at a counter, obviously eager to make a score, but…

"This Flying Lady is newish and common," he said, taking a classic Rolls-Royce hood ornament from the box, "but what the heck, I'll give you fifteen bucks for it."

"Can't do fifteen, Ferret. Dumbo scored that beauty at an estate sale—so he says—for thirty green ones. They go for four-to-five hundred on eBay."

"Only the vintage models, Easy, but okay, no deal on the Lady, but…These six old baseballs are all skinned-up and dirty, but… What the heck, Katie says throwing a ball back and forth with our boy, Ray Ray, would be good for father-and-son bonding. I'll give you five bucks for the lot."

"Now that you mention it, Ferret, my nephew has enrolled in Little League," she said, reaching for a still-white ball. "I'd better keep that clean one, which will leave you with five."

"No, no, Easy," he said, holding back the box. "Ray Ray is, uh, completely uncoordinated and will be throwing balls over my head. So I need 'em all, and… What the heck, I'll go ten bucks."

"Chasing after overthrown balls will be good exercise for you, Garrett. I'll just hang on to that whitish one."

"No, uh, see, Rhonda, Ray Ray is, uh, almost blind and would have a hard time seeing these dirty balls, so…Tell you what, you can keep the three dirtiest ones and I'll go up to fifteen for the other three."

"Make it thirty bucks and you've got a deal."

As Ferret Rutledge scurried out the door with the box of three balls in hand, Rhonda had no pang of conscience. Her fellow scavenger had brought out the Flying Lady as a diversionary tactic, then clearly made a point of seeming to not notice, just as she herself had made a point to not mention, the handwriting on the whitest ball. Yes, she herself had done the scribbling, but made no representation whatsoever that the famous someone named "Mickey Mantle" had autographed the baseball: *For my best buddy.*

And as Dumbo often quoted someone as having said, "You can't con a completely honest man."

CHAPTER 3

Returned from a clinic after loaning his mom's brown Buick boiler to Dumbo Dumphy—that was how partners in big deals rolled with one another when emergencies reared ugly heads—Max leaned back in his office chair and counted turkeys, so to speak. Interest earned on his savings account was chicken feed compared to what Dumbo would do with the nest egg. By Thanksgiving, if not sooner, Yours Truly would be soaked in giblet gravy.

And other fat butterballs were sure to follow. Dumbo was a natural-born wheeler-dealer, with a sharp eye for…

"Yo, Mr. Maximo," said the teenaged kid who—like a Dr. Watson did for Sherlock Holmes and others had done for other famous gumshoes—jotted case reports for him. "Any crime afoot that deserves our attention?"

"Nah, only a penny-ante shoplifting caper. Cops in hot pursuit. Nothing the local Barney Fife's can't handle on their own."

"Oh," said the kid, returning a small notebook to a shirt pocket and a pencil to behind a stuck-out ear, then crossing his arms in an obviously selfish fit of what good writers would call pique.

His jotter had been sending case reports to a bigtime publisher on the west coast, but *Maximo Morgan Mysteries* seemed to not be selling like even lukewarm cakes. In fact, not only was Yours Truly yet to see one thin dime for write-ups of his dickwork, he was also yet to be pestered by a single fan wanting to take a so-called selfie picture with him. The kid just didn't have the "right stuff" to make case reports gripping to readers. The time had come for him to go to the mound, so to speak, relieve his "pitcher" from further duty, and…

"For the next big lay that comes along, I'm thinking of hiring a pro to jot the record," Max blurted. "I need a 'Mickey Spillane', who knows how to get a grip."

"Mr. Mike Hammer's case report jotter bought the farm years ago, Mr. Maximo. Same for Mr. Dashiell Hammett and all the other jotters who wrote up gumshoe case reports back in the *Noir*. Most of today's pros are dames, and…Nothing personal, Mr. Maximo, but unless you paid a desperate broad big bucks…"

"That'll be no *problemo*," said Max, who then—itching to flaunt—went on to put the kid wise to the big deal Dumbo Dumphy and he were hatching.

"Bottom line: Opportunity is knocking loud and clear for investment in high-tech reinvention of a wheel, so to speak."

"Gee, I dunno," said the kid, squirming in his chair after Yours Truly put him in the know. "I was in second or third grade at the time, but recall reading a case report about…Square manhole covers? Sounds like the exact same get-rich-quick idea Wilford Wiggins pitched to kids in the Rover Avenue neighborhood…"

A lowdown "Wilford Wiggins" glommed Dumbo's idea?

"…until Encyclopedia Brown pointed out that round covers don't fall into manholes no matter which way they're turned, that they take less material to make, and that millions of round holes are already in place."

Encyclopedia Brown again! Max was sick-and-tired of hearing about a kid detective called "Encyclopedia" because he supposedly knew so much about so many things. Supposedly when only a teenager, Brown set up a detective agency and got cases written up by…

"Maybe we should do it that way, Mr. Maximo. I could solve cases, and you could do the jotting, like a Mr. Donald J. Sobol did for Encyclopedia Brown."

Max dropped the soft soap and sent the kid to the showers, so to speak.

Dad-gum-it, thousands if not millions of round manhole

covers went missing every year because they were easy to roll. Yeah, a few square covers might fall into holes if not properly handled, and yeah, existing manholes were round, but so what? Time and high technology marched on. In the old-fashioned past, slow-footed dummies like the kid thought air travel would never catch on because planes sometimes crashed and every city would have to have an airport.

As for the cockamamie idea of switching roles—with the snot-nosed brat setting up a Brown Detective Agency and Yours Truly doing the jotting—fuggetaboutit. Even when he got to soaking in a warm tub of gravy, Maximo Morgan would still be his name and private dicking would still be his game.

CHAPTER 4

Willis V. Willis sat with feet on his desk, ruing his choice of the long and bumpy career path he had followed. Growing up, he had wanted to be a farmer, but his mother had a long-standing grudge against a door-to-door salesman who had yoked her with lifetime magazine subscriptions, and so…Willis sighed. He had become a country lawyer, plying his craft in a storefront office across the street from the county courthouse in the small town of Okmulgee, Oklahoma. After almost forty years of pettifogging…

Willis again sighed.

He was now into his sixties, with squat to show for his labors in the vineyard of human misfortune. To feather his own bed for a comfortable retirement, he needed to find a bird's nest on the ground, one of those personal injury cases—preferably involving death—that paid contingency fees up to 35% of damages awarded to clients out of the deep pockets of insurance companies. That was the kind of get-rich-quick opportunity he needed to fall from a tree.

But gas was not cheap. Driving around all day, listening for the sound of ambulance sirens was expensive, and tiresome. Racing against other attorneys to accident scenes was dangerous. In other words, damnit, whereas practice of law used to be a dignified profession governed by a code of ethics, nowadays lawyering had sunk below used car sales to the level of running for political office.

It was downright disgraceful how cable tv shows were now constantly interrupted by commercial appearances of legal hacks self-identified as "The Hammer"…"The Strong Arm"…"The

Heavy Hitter" …"The Avenger"…shouting about how they would "Push! Pound! Punish!" reckless drivers and insurance companies…"hunt them down, rip out their hearts, make 'em pay"… promising that everyone who called their toll-free numbers would get what they deserved.

All bragged about huge amounts they'd won for clients. One even posted a price list of likely awards ranging from $179,738.63 for a broken back to $289, 999.95 for a fractured skull to multi-millions per dead body. Another vowed that even if an auto accident was his client's fault, he would make sure the other party's greedy insurance company paid through the nose. For a guy to get his own snout into a trough for trial lawyers such as the one slopped by congress to pay off victims of so-called bad Camp Lejeune water dating back to the 1950s, he had to start with a million-dollar advertising budget.

As a small town lawyer on his own, all Willis could afford were a few local bus bench signs with his name, number and…

"Are you The LitiGATOR?" said a man's voice. "Are you Willis 'Versus' Willis, the lawyer who 'eats 'em alive'?"

Willis looked up. Standing in the opened doorway was a middle-aged, ginger-haired, shrimp-sized fella, wearing a neck brace.

"Depends how you got that injury," he said to the walk-in. "If you're being divorced by a neck-wringing wife, the answer is that I have no appetite for penny-ante…"

"Nah, Easy ain't easy—not anymore—but she knows better than to haul me into court. And it would be a waste of time for me to file for a fair split against her. I got rear-ended by a rich old lady recklessly driving a classic Rolls-Royce."

Rolls-Royce? Willis took his feet off the desk and invited the prospective client to have a seat across from him. "Broken neck?" he asked. "Fractured skull? Any chance of death resulting?"

"Suffering from whiplash," was the shrimp's disappointing reply, "but… Now that you mention it, Willis, I am having headaches in addition to pain in my neck, along with dizziness that could lead to fatal brain damage."

Hmmm. Except for the walk-in being still alive, the opportunity to make a killing seemed almost too good to be true, and that usually turned out to be the case.

"I'm awful busy at the moment, Mr…"

"Clark Dumphy, but everyone calls me Dumbo on account of my ears."

"Sorry, Mr. Dumphy, but like I say, I'm awful…"

"And like I say, Willis: rich old lady driving a Rolls. Piece of cake. No need for you to roll up sleeves and put a shoulder to the wheel. All you have to do is write a letter or two. I've already lined up a private investigator to do the legwork. Max Morgan, a real go-getter, will be on it like white on rice."

Max Morgan was the mailman down the road in the town of Henryetta. Willis had used the postal employee through the years to provide forwarding addresses for deadbeat husbands and such. After Morgan set up shop as as "Maximo Morgan, the Fat Man" he had engaged the so-called private detective — still for a Christmas ham in lieu of fee — to track down a runaway wife.

The "go-getter" had found his client's wandering spouse alright, but gave her the impression that he, her abandoned husband's attorney, was in possession of "pots-and-pans" — divorce lawyer lingo for marital assets — worth fifty thousand dollars. She had come after the goods and almost killed him when it turned out that the client's foot locker entrusted to his keeping contained, in fact, only cookware.

"I'd have to have an up-front retainer of, say, ten thousand American dollars to drop other cases from my docket," said Willis, "plus 35% of any and all damages ultimately awarded."

"For writing a couple of letters?! That's steep for rolling off a log, Willis, but… Your bus bench sign has got me sold. Since I'm a little short of cash at the moment, tell you what: straight contingency fee of 50% of the take and you've got a deal. It'll be like shooting a fish in a barrel."

Hmmm.

Willis had to admit that whiplash caused by a rear-ending by a rich old lady driving a Rolls-Royce sure enough looked like something on the ground worth stooping for.

CHAPTER 5

Ankling across the Dean Motor Company's used car lot, Max made a point to not even glance at any of the rides lined up in rows. Visually "kicking tires" would have been a tip-off that he was in the market to buy. Yeah, he was born at night, but not last night. No way was Yours Truly going to be played for a rube who had just then fell off a truck of turnips. To get the ball rolling he would put a cover story in play, then wait for a high-pressure salesman to make the first move.

Inside an on-site hut… "Max Morgan," he said, extending a hand to a beefy guy for a shake. "Happened to be ankling by and wondered if anyone around here would like to attend a meeting of butterfly collectors next Tuesday night at…"

"Randy Grimes, Senior Sales Manager," said the guy, shaking. "And you betcha, Max. I myself love to pin butterflies. Where and exactly when…?"

"Uh, time and place not yet set, but since I happen to be passing by…Hmmm, I happen to remember I've been thinking of trading in the family's 2008 Buick *LaCrosse*—four doors, brown, low mileage—for a roomier set of wheels."

"A *LaCrosse*, you say. Yeah, that's a mid-size and, pardon me happening to notice, Max, you're not. But they don't make the *LaCrosse* in North America anymore. Most already in junkyards. Too ugly. Cheap plastic interior. Front-wheel drive and magnetic steering makes it easy for old ladies to change lanes and park, but otherwise…I recall one of the car magazines describing the 2008 *LaCrosse* as looking like a 1996 *Regal* with a fugly grille."

Skating from bait to switch…"Actually the Buick is my mom's

boiler," said Max. "Mom doesn't drive much anymore, but — now that I think about it — she might want to keep the brown skates for sentimental reasons. At the right price, I might be willing to tap into my U.S. Postal Service Pension Fund and pay cash for one of your..."

"Sorry," said the high-pressure salesman, "none of our vehicles are for sale."

Not for sale? For crying out loud, through a large window Max now saw that every car on the lot had a price on its windshield in two-foot-high numbers.

"All already spoken for," said the Senior Sales Manager. "Due to supply-chain bottlenecks, demand for pre-owned vehicles — at any price — has gone through the roof."

In a lowered voice, Max put Randy Grimes wise to the fact that he would soon be rolling in dough. In other words, at any price and then some was no *problemo*. After some further artful haggling, sure enough...

"Well, Max, seeing as how you're a high roller," said Grimes, folding like an unstarched shirt, "I do happen to have a recent, uh, repossessed vehicle out back that you might be interested in."

Bingo.

Ankling out a backdoor into a lot behind the sales office...

"No, the vintage Rolls is the personal car of Mr. Dean's son, a playboy you might say. He brought it in to be waxed and... Don't touch the Flying Lady!" the salesman barked, referring to the ride's fancy chrome hood ornament in the shape of a woman wearing a windswept gown and seeming to be in the process of taking flight.

"Officially, the radiator mascot is called 'Spirit of Ecstasy'," the salesman then said, with what looked to be a leerish look in his eyes. "And before that she was known as 'The Whisperer', due to her holding a finger to her lips. See, heh, heh, heh, for his personal Rolls back in 1909, a married Lord So-and-So had her sculpted to look like his secret lover, and...Don't touch her!"

Ooops! The Flying Lady disappeared down into the vehicle's radiator.

"It's an automatic security device built into Rolls-Royces, designed to make the Lady impossible for a common thief to steal. Give up on her, Morgan. Step over here for a look at something more in your, uh, style."

Thirty minutes later…

Honk. Honk. Honk.

Max could hardly wait to see the look on his mom's face.

Honk. Honk. Honk.

Her old brown Buick boiler was a gas-guzzling clunker.

Honk. Honk. Honk.

The two of them needed affordable and comfortable wheels.

Honk. Honk…

Finally, Mom came out the front door of the frame house they shared. She squinted in his direction as though unable to believe her own eyes.

"Hop in for a spin!" he hollered through an open driver's-side window of the new family wheels. "Let's drag Main."

After rolling her eyes, Mom warily trudged across the front lawn and said: "What is it, Max? A school bus?"

"Attractively yellow alright, and roomy enough to haul a bunch of kids to school and back. But no, this honey is a custom-built *Cafenero Coach*, previously owned by a Russian oligarch and seized by Uncle Sam."

"But…But…But there are traces of paint on the side that say *Taxico Tacos*, and a food-service window."

"All the better for letting light into the roomy interior. Climb in, Mom. This baby doesn't have little bucket seats; it has hundred-gallon barrel seats in front and bean bags in the rear. Plus a freezer, griddle, deep fat fryer and…"

"Where is my brown boiler, Max?"

"Not to worry, Mom. Randy Grimes, Senior Sales Manager at the Dean Motor Company used car lot accepted a blank promissory note…"

"You signed a blank promissory note?"

"…and said he would fill-in the trade-in amount soon as Dumbo returns the clunker."

"You traded in…? You entrusted my brown Buick *LaCrosse* to Darlene Dumphy's untrustworthy son?!"

Untrustworthy?

After dragging him by an ear into the house and setting him down at the kitchen table, Mom explained that Mrs. Dumphy had been bragging at this morning's yoga class about how Dumbo had raised the cash to buy a chain of dry cleaners in Tulsa by pulling what was called a Baltimore Stockbroker trick, to-wit:

Dumbo had sent out notices to eighty clients of a Tulsa stock brokerage firm, half touting a certain stock and half warning that the stock price would go down. A week later he sent notices to the forty clients who had bought or sold the stock based on him being right, twenty notices touting another stock and twenty panning it. And so it went for a total of six weeks until his advice to a single investor had proven to be consistently right on the money. To that lucky guy he had pitched a big deal to buy the chain of dry cleaners and…

"Yeah that's Dumbo, always on a roll."

"Max, Darlene Dumphy admitted that the Christian Brothers Cleaners chain has gone bankrupt. Dumbo left the investor holding an empty bag."

Well, so what? No one hit a home run seven times in a row.

"No, especially not Dumbo Dumphy, who struck out six times in a row, but made that poor investor unwisely think otherwise."

Hmmm. Max decided now was not the right time to brag that he had almost emptied his savings account to invest in Dumbo's square manhole cover venture.

TUESDAY

September 9, 2025

CHAPTER 6

"It's not about money," said Dumbo, shaking hands to wrap up a power-breakfast meeting, during which Max had happily agreed to work *Case of Who's That Lady*. "It's about accountability, and keeping our streets safe for kids. Look at the late Jerry Lewis. Already rich and famous, the King of Comedy went out there onto that stage year after year to 'break a leg' for crippled children."

That was Dumbo, a successful businessman with a big heart in the right place and, uh, smallish feet still on the ground, a guy with ambition to do well, yeah, but also to do good.

For instance, in one recent venture that he'd modestly mentioned—Curb Crawlers Corps—Dumbo had hired troubled youths who had been kicked to the curb by society. Equipped with buckets of paint, brushes and cardboard stencils, the juvenile delinquents were given the opportunity, not to get off the streets exactly, but to work at painting addresses on curbs—to make it easier and safer for police, fireman and other emergency vehicles to know where they were—then going to doors of homeowners and asking to be paid for their community service.

"Most decent folks will fork over forty or fifty bucks for a good cause," Dumbo had said over scrambled eggs and bacon, "especially when the alternative is to have the addresses painted-over in solid black, which tends to spoil a house's curb appeal."

After ankling side-by-side from the Wide-O-Wake Cafe, Max reached into a pants pocket for a newly withdrawn wad of bills, but…Dumbo was no cheapskate.

"Don't even think about reimbursing me for the cash outlays," said his new best friend. "It's the least I can do in appreciation for the long-term loan of your former family auto."

Dumbo was referring to his cost of replacing the brown boiler's tires that rode rough during his drive to Okmulgee yesterday on account of too much tread, and also the cost of replacing the wheels that had wobbled on his way back due to misfit tires.

"Hold onto your cash for that venture we discussed," the generous wheeler-dealer added, with a slap on the back. "We've gotta get your own good works the attention they deserve."

Max climbed into the parked *Cafenero*, fired up its two hundred horses, and—in a cloud of diesel smoke—set out to find the little old lady who had taken flight after rear-ending Dumbo yesterday. Clueless local police had whizzed right by the wreckage without noticing, and by the time he himself got back from wrapping up their square manhole cover venture while riding with his partner to a clinic, the little old lady's big red muscle car had also disappeared.

Arrived at what a large rusted sign identified as ROCCO'S BODY SHOP & AUTO SALVAGE, he got out of and down from the *Cafenero*, then ankled toward a junkyard protected by a high chainlink fence topped with swirling razor wire. At a gate signed ENTER AT OWN RISK …

Grrrrr…

For crying out loud, inside the junkyard only a heavy-duty steel chain saved him from bloody assault by a lunging dog.

Grrrrrrr…

"Down, Leroy! Down Leroy Brown!" shouted a grizzled old codger, coming out of a hut clad entirely in automobile hubcaps.

Leroy Brown? Namesake of Encyclopedia Brown?

Grrrrrrrr…

"Bad, bad Leroy Brown is meaner than ol' King Kong," said the cagy codger, coming closer. "What's your bidness, mister?"

Grrrrrrrrrr…

"Here to have a look at the newish big red muscle wheels you might have towed from the scene of a Main Street collision yesterday."

"Wheels? I don't tow wheels."

Grrrrrrrrr…

"I mean the whole muscle car, buster," Max said to the oldtimer, who was obviously playing dumb.

"You mean a newish, say, Chrysler 300? I never towed in no such car."

Grrrrrrrrrrrr…

"Oh yeah, let's just have a look to make sure."

"Why?"

"Let's just say Yours Truly is curious," said Max, taking a light green gratuity from his wallet.

After walking through a maze of wrecked vehicles…bingo.

"That's no muscle car. That's a Rolls-Royce," said the possibly truly dumb salvage yard operator, standing right next to a large red car lacking a Flying Lady hood ornament.

"And I didn't trade-out any parts," he added. "The tires were bald and the wheels mismatched when I picked up the Rolls."

Yeah, probably the savvy car owner had made those changes for a smoother, less wobbly ride, Max imagined.

He glanced at the barely dented front, then detected a round hole in the car's hood. Hmmm. Maybe the wheels were a Rolls. Maybe the Flying Lady had fallen into the radiator. He looked into the hole, but…no soap.

"I didn't take off the other chrome decorations or the catalytic converter neither".

Max opened a door, leaned inside the mysterious vehicle, noticed that the steering wheel had been jolted to the right side and…

"I took out the radio for safe keeping."

After wedging himself into the front seat, he was disappointed not to find, say, illegal drugs stashed in the glove box instead of a certificate indicating that…By golly, the big red rear-ender was in fact a 2016 Rolls-Royce, insured by Lone Star Insurance Company and…bingo…owned by a Lady Booth-Montjoy.

"The radio is in the office, under lock and key."

With his hands feeling between lush seat cushions, Max half-hoped to touch the hard cold steel of some kind of weapon, but no, he dug out only what looked to be dog or cat hair.

"I've got the keys to the trunk right here on my ring," said the keeper of the pricey ride, leading him to the vehicle's rear. "The ring never leaves my belt, day or night. Just ask the wife."

The lid of the trunk popped open and… Hmmm. No spare tire, but…

"Don't look at me. This is the first time I've opened the rear end."

Max detected what looked to be women's clothes stashed in the trunk. Rummaging through garments on one side, he noted that all were shabby and obviously old, but…

"Look, buddy, I don't want no trouble."

…dresses, handbags and belts lodged into the other side…

"There's no need to call the cops."

…were all brand new glad rags and…

"What'll it take for you to forget you were here?"

…price tags were still attached.

Max accepted return of the light green gratuity waved by the old codger, and did the math. Yeah, it added up: Lady Booth-Montjoy, a local celebrity of sorts, had been shopping shortly before rear-ending Dumbo's little car.

Trudging back to the junkyard gate, the hamster he sometimes imagined inside his head began to spin a wheel.

Grrrrr…

No one could have gotten past Leroy Brown to steal parts off the Rolls when the guard dog was likely unchained after hours and…

Grrrrrrrrr…

It hit him like a pie in the face. Yeah, he must have understandably mistaken the big red rear-ender for a muscle car because it had no gaudy hood ornament when it crashed into Dumbo's little MINI Cooper yesterday morning and…

It struck Max as strange as fiction was said to be that a rich old woman such as Lady Booth-Montjoy would drive around in a Rolls-Royce with its fancy hood ornament and other chrome missing.

Hmmm.

Yeah, plot was thickening like cornbread mix in the re-named *Case of <u>Where's</u> That Lady?*

CHAPTER 7

After again running traps—this time checking for goods in six heavy-duty cardboard donation bins scattered around town—Rhonda parked her pickup out front of her Easy Pickens What-n-Whatnot Shop. Again, pickins had been slim. If sharing was caring, people nowadays just didn't give a damn about supporting fellow human beings, or local businesses.

Okay, the bins somewhat resembled the ones used by Goodwill Industries. Yes, heart-shaped signs referred to "Goods from and for People of Goodwill". Other signage expressly asked good people to donate secondhand clothing, shoes, handbags, belts, hats, linens, books, household appliances and whatnot for a good cause, but so what? Recycling unwanted things was good for the environment. Charges for overhead and handling were justified. Hustling to make a buck here and there was the American Way.

For crying out loud, a sleazy bins operator in Oklahoma City used a similar red shield and nickname for the Salvation Army to stock a chain of used goods stores called "Sally Ann's Closet".

Inside her shop, Rhonda sighed. Merch was thin, not entirely due to recent sales volume. Supply was also a problem, but… With little reason to open for business, she locked the door behind her and hurried to a small back room that served as her office. At her desk, she fired up her computer and went to the *Acorns-to-Oaks Family Tree* site.

According to *ABC News* and *Time Magazine*, genealogy was now second only to gardening in popularity as a so-called pastime. Internet traffic at websites catering to interest in finding ancestors was said to be second only to those devoted to pornography. Supposedly the newfound fascination with knowing about bygone family members had to do with better understanding one's self, but…

In Rhonda's view, the appeal of the fad was not the "knowing" but the "doing" of genealogy. She sensed that to most the "hobby" was like a treasure hunt of sorts, based on hope of discovering a relationship to a famous person of the past and/or association with a self-described prestigious group such as Daughters of the American Revolution. More intriguing to many was the possibility of encountering a puzzle or mystery, even if the solution did not necessarily reflect glory upon a family connection. With that idea in mind…

♫ *Genealogy/I am doing it/ genealogy…* ♫

As a children's song of long ago echoed inside her head, Rhonda randomly clicked on a posting and read:

MOTLEY FAMILY
Archibald Riggs Motley m.Rebecca Bodine
b. 1/21/ 1822-3 12/24/ 1845b. 8/21/ 1827
d. 7/25/ 1869d. 2/03/ 1860
Franklin Bates MotleyWilliam James Motley
Clarabel Motley
b. 3/22 / 1841 b. 3/31/ 18/44 b. 4/01 /1850
♫ *Genealogy/ I am doing genealogy…* ♫
William James Motley m.Sarah Blaine(w)
b. 3/31/ 1844 6/30/ 1864 b. 7/27/ 1844
d. 9/26/ 1899 d. 2/14/ 2004
Wanda Sue Blaine

Scrolling down, she noted numerous posts by various people, most named Motley, inquiring about first names, marriages, births and deaths of kinfolk.

♫ *And the reasons why I'm doing it are very clear to me…* ♫

Rhonda then reached into a cardboard box sitting on the floor beside her desk. Old bibles were plentiful online and cheap. The one she plucked from the box…Perfect, an American

Bible Society specimen published in 1860… and not marred by personal notations.

♫ *Genealogy/ I am doing genealogy…* ♫

On a yellowed page at the front, she copied the names, births and deaths data of Motley family "acorns". Turned to a page ornately headed MARRIAGES, she wrote with an antique fountain pen:

William James Motley wed Widow Sarah Blaine on June…

Buzz. Buzz. Buzzzzz…

With another sigh, Rhonda put down the pen. At the shop's front door…

"Bad news and good news!" said her friend, Clarise Kilpatrick, rushing through the doorway. "Bad news for me," the so-called Lone Lawyer said. "By the time I got to Vultures Row in Okmulgee late yesterday, Dumbo was coming out of the office of Willis V. Willis, with a smile on his face. But that's very good news for you, Easy."

Clarise explained that Willis V. Willis, known as "The LitiGATOR", was a wise old reptile who lurked in weeds, snapped up only sure-fire cases and, "even better", never risked actually going to trial. "He has probably already filed a lawsuit against the rich old lady who bumped into Dumbo," she said. "But mark my words, Easy, by day after tomorrow The LitiGATOR will settle the case with an insurance company for hundreds of thousands of dollars, if not millions!"

Rhonda ground her teeth, hardly able to believe that Dumbo might get so lucky at playing the oldest short con in the book and stumbling into a pay-off equal to or greater than what he could only have dreamed of scoring for play of a long con. Her husband wouldn't share the windfall. Damnit, for supporting her ne'er-do-well spouse and his cockeyed get-rich-schemes during more than twenty years of married misery, she deserved…

"So I am free to represent you!" her old friend exclaimed. "For myself, at just my regular low hourly rate, but it will be an orgasmic pleasure to snatch at least half the prize from Dumbo's hands for you. *Carpe diem*, Easy. Divorce that low-life grifter tomorrow!"

For the nth time, but now seriously, Rhonda promised Clarise she would sleep on filing for divorce, which sent the het up attorney out the door to "draw up papers", but…Among other concerns about taking legal action, she would have to discuss the matter with her grown daughters. Both had for years urged her to dump their deadbeat dad, but neither understood what could be at stake.

♫ *Genealogy/ I am doing genealogy…* ♫

Back at her desk with fountain pen back in hand, Rhonda read:

MARRIAGES
William James Motley wed Widow Sarah Blaine on June…

Completing the entry, another inspirational song about genealogy popped into her head. To pique buyer interest at a maximum price, her eBay listing of the "Motley Family Bible" would need a tantalizing hook.

Hmmm.

♫ *It was many many years ago when I was twenty-three* ♫ she heard the voice of Willie Nelson sing. ♫ *I was married to a widow, she' was pretty as can be…* ♫

Rhonda referred to the Motley Family chart on her computer screen, turned to a bible page headed BIRTHS, and wrote:

Wanda Sue Blaine was born on July 4, 1860, and adopted by William James Motley on July 1,1864.

Rollo Edward Motley was born on March16,1865.

♫ *This widow had a grown-up daughter with flaming hair of red/ My father fell in love with her, and soon the two were wed…* ♫

Hmmm.

♫ *This made my dad my son-law and changed my very life/ My daughter was my mother 'cause she was my father's wife…* ♫

Rhonda scribed that Archibald Riggs Motley married his adopted granddaughter, Wanda Sue Blaine.

After then making several more intertwined entries consistent with both the twisted lyrics of the old Willie Nelson song and the Tennessee backwoods background of the Motley family, she leaned back in her chair and LOL'd, tickled to imagine a current family member paying three hundred dollars, reading the scripted bible pages, and wailing:

♫*Archibald Riggs Motley was his own grandpa/ It sounds silly, I know, but it really is so/ He was his own grandpa*♫

CHAPTER 8

The roly-poly kid again sat across from Max,, sent to his copy shop office by the high school Principal to apologize for stealing a stapler. As it turned out, the paper-clipper had only been temporarily mislaid in the workstation's desk drawer. So…

"Sorry about the bum rap, kid," said Max, "but what the heck, now that you're here, I've decided to take you back as my case report jotter."

Without a word of gratitude, the kid just sat there with arms folded across his chest.

"Yeah, working the lay now re-re-re-named *Case of a Dangerous Old Lady*, and it's moving ahead quicker than green grass passing through the goose that lays golden eggs."

"Dangerous old lady?"

"A rear-ender who…"

"Rear-ender ?"

"…crashed her fancy red Rolls-Royce into the backside of my business partner. Too many horses under the hood for a little old lady to handle. The good news is that Yours Truly is in line to indirectly cash-in on the outcome by lending a hand to Dumbo Dumphy, who has come up with another idea to invest…"

"Sorry, Mr. Maximo, I'm not interested in jotting details of a routine investigation related to a simple insurance claim. My ambition is to become famous like Dr. Watson, for helping to solve crimes, writing up reports of gripping cases involving hardboiled private dickery, and someday—as you know—walk in my own gumshoes like Ms. Jessica Fletcher."

"Wise up kid. Ever hear the oldtime radio accounts of cases

worked by Johnny Dollar back in the *Noir*, or see the post-*Noir* tv documentaries of Thomas Banacek's private dicking? Dollar and Banacek worked exclusively as insurance investigators, and were not softboiled, not by a long shot. Both were savvy P.I.s who… It was Banacek who coined the old Polish proverb I adopted as a motto, quote: 'Though the hippopotamus has no sting in his tail, a wise man would prefer to be sat upon by a bee.'"

"Yeah, but Mr. Dollar and Mr. Banacek worked on the side of insurance companies to solve criminal cases of insurance fraud committed by hustlers that almost always ended up also involving murrrderrr," the nit-picking kid pointed out. "If there was any crime going down in your case, Mr. Maximo, you would be on the wrong side as a…as a duped accomplice."

Duped accomplice?

"Nobody dupes Maximo Morgan," said Max, before setting the kid straight. "Yours Truly has been around the roller rink a few times, knows the score, and has the streetwise moxie to not be taken in by any two-bit hustler. Besides, working *Case of a Dangerous Old Lady* gets another foot in a door," he explained. "In appreciation for Yours Truly gumshoeing in, okay, an only semi-criminal insurance case, Dumbo — that's Mr. Dumphy to you — wants to make sure my good works get the attention they deserve by…Get this: we're gonna dump that no-account west coast publisher you've been sending case reports to, and roll out *Maximo Morgan Mysteries* ourselves!"

"Wow!" said the kid, rising part-way out of his chair like a semi-stuck overweight Jack-in-a-Box. "That phony out there in L.A. who edits my jottings, mainly by adding flowery adjectives, is to blame for the *Maximo Morgan Mysteries* that nobody finds gripping, but still gets to be semi-famous if not rich. William LeRoy is just a wannabe James Patterson in my book, without the marketing know-how."

Max drew a blank.

The kid, now up on his feet, went on to piss-and-moan that the Patterson guy was an ad agency writer of slogans back in the 1970s, who took up jotting cop case reports on the side, and got lucky. After supposedly authoring book after book on practically a weekly basis, he had been forced to come clean, and now admitted that he'd had the help of "co-authors". In total, 300 to 400 million copies of Patterson "branded" books had been sold.

Max's ears perked up.

"So count me in, Mr. Maximo. Getting sprung from the closet and seeing my name on the cover of a gripping *Maximo Morgan Mystery* will be a dream come true."

Name on the cover? Hmmm.

Like the kid himself had said, Jessica Fletcher wrote up her own case reports for books and tv documentaries. How hard could typing be? And after all, Max noted out loud, Yours Truly would be taking out another loan on his U.S. Postal Service Pension to set up the publishing venture.

"Why would you do that, Mr. Maximo? So-called vanity publishers will put my jottings into book form, and charge only about six percent of sales to print them. All you have to do is come up with gripping criminal cases for me to help solve and write up."

Hmmm. Max did arithmetic.

"For you to put up your own money, Mr. Max, well, ever listen to the recordings of that oldtime radio show called *Bunco Squad*?"

"Remind me," said Max, without interest.

"The program dramatized cases picked out of police files from around the country and always started with a Captain Trumble warning: 'So you think you're smart, that you're nobody's fool. Brother, you can be taken. The bunco artist, the swindler, the con man: he comes in a thousand disguises, he has a million tricks. He can make a sucker out of you. BE ON YOUR GUARD!'"

Max's mind remained elsewhere.

"A Chief of Police in the recorded case report I listened to a couple of weeks ago said that particular Bunco Squad bust exposed one of the most vicious swindles ever attempted in St. Louis," the kid pointlessly continued. "And Captain Trumble ended the program by warning that the same bunco scheme was being tried in other places, including Oklahoma City. Of course, that was back in the *Noir*, but still…"

Max's mind was on getting rich and famous.

"The scheme was a Book Worm Bunco, in which a so-called professor from out of town flashed a manuscript he claimed to have jotted, and conned a gullible old couple into putting their life savings into cutting out a bigtime publisher and printing the text themselves. Turned out the 'professor' had only typed up a copy of a school book that had been around for years. So I'm just saying, Mr. Maximo: BE ON YOUR GUARD!"

Hmmm.

Max noodled: Why not do the jotting of *Case of a Dangerous Old Lady* himself, bring in the Patterson guy to put in a few catchy adjectives for grippage and have Dumbo grease the marketing wheels? At, say, five bucks a pop, sales of even a million copies would…

"Kid, you may have a bright future ahead of you," said Max, "but on second thought, to put it gently, not as a case jotter for the publishing venture Dumbo and I are setting up. Sorry, that's how the wheels of bigtime business roll. No tears."

CHAPTER 9

Beside a public water fountain inside an Okmulgee County Courthouse corridor, Willis lay in wait for Judge Tim "Two-Putt" Dwight to come out of his chambers. The crotchety old judge was renowned for his impatience, which was why Willis had expressly reminded the Court Clerk of the many hams he had provided for Christmases past. By getting the case of *Clark Dumphy vs. Lady Booth-Montjoy* assigned to Dwight, he reckoned he had won half the battle, or rather, had possibly avoided half the battle of full-bore litigation.

Going to trial would take a lot of work. No doubt the defendant's insurance company would intervene as a party to the lawsuit, making the process lengthy, stressful, and the outcome uncertain, especially if either other party opted to have a jury decide matters allegedly in dispute. Jurors might not like Clark Dumphy, they might not like witnesses called in support of his case. Hell, they might not like his lawyer. Despite the glorification of American jurisprudence, putting the simplest of cases in the hands of Dumphy's peers would be like handing over the controls of a spaceship to…to people like Dumphy. Judges were marginally more intelligent, equally important, and more predictable.

For instance, Judge Dwight was known to be an avid sports fan, and an equally avid golfer, as evidenced by old photos on a wall of his chambers: one showing Babe Ruth, not in New York Yankee pinstripes but in golfing garb, the other a picture of the entrance to a underpass beneath a section of the Bronx River Parkway in Eastchester, New York, identified by plaque as "The

Babe's Shortcut".

Dwight delighted in explaining that members of a Leewood Country Club had financed construction of the tunnel in order cut a half hour off Ruth's rush from their golf course to games at Yankee Stadium. With even more relish, he often quoted a famous golfer of yesteryear named Gene Sarazen to the effect that Ruth was as good a golfer as he was a baseball player, for nine holes played in two hours—which happened to be the average length of major league baseball games back then—after which he seemed to lose interest.

The judge interpreted that factoid as proof that the four hours typically required for a group of four to play a round of golf was too long by half. Noting also that individual players taking fewer or more than two-putts to finish a hole was atypical—and wasted up to two hours per round—he made of a practice of granting to other golfers and taking for himself "two-putt gimmes" and thus acquired his nickname. After rushing to a next hole, he would insist on "playing through" slow groups ahead as a matter of right. And on the bench displayed similar intolerance for…

"Your Honor!" Willis shouted, as Judge Dwight bolted from his chambers and hurried toward a courthouse exit, likely bound for a golf course. Chasing after him, "I just want to give you a heads up that I have filed a personal injury lawsuit and the clerk assigned the case to your docket. It's a simple matter that…"

His Honor stopped in his tracks, wheeled around, and said: "Aw shit, Willis, can't you settle the sumbitch?"

Before he could further explain…

"I suppose you've got that wordy sawbones from the Docs On Wheels Clinic lined up to give expert testimony. Hell if Doc 'Mettenblahblah' and other members of the medical profession spent as much time treating patients in hospitals as shilling for fees in court, eyes of the blind would be opened, ears of the deaf would be unstopped, and the lame would be leaping like deer as biblically prophesied."

"As a matter of fact, the plaintiff suffers from whiplash and Dr. Mettenbaugh has agreed to…"

"And, damnit, if Lone Star happens to be the insurance company involved, a trial would mean hours of bullshit about fine print shoveled by so-called 'Big Game Bob' Huckaby from Texas."

"Regrettably, Lone Star does happen to be the defendant's insurance company. But, Judge, it's a simple open-and-shut case with no pertinent facts credibly in dispute. My investigator, Max Morgan, has identified the defendant, driver of the other car, as a wealthy old woman who no doubt…"

"Morgan?! Aw shit! Prospect of having that babbling idiot on the stand takes the rag off the bush. Settle the sumbitch, damnit!"

"That is my devout intent, Your Honor. In fact, to save the Court's time, I have filed a Motion for Summary Judgement. With the defendant's liability established, reaching an out-of-court settlement with Huckaby on amount of damages will be still difficult, but certain, without taking Your Honor's time. If you would see fit to, uh, tee-up the matter on tomorrow's motion docket, well, I know it's short notice, but…"

"Nonsense! Justice delayed is justice denied. We'll play through the other pettifoggers making bullshit motions, and move on."

Though not a golfer himself, Willis silently congratulated himself for shots well played, so to speak. With his ball now on the putting surface, also so to speak, he was reasonably confident that at tomorrow's hearing on his Motion for Summary Judgement—knock on wood—Judge "Two Putt" Dwight would grant a "gimme". On the other hand…

Willis sensed a headache coming on.

He'd heard of a term—"rub of the green"—as descriptive of inexplicable turns of events on golf courses, and had noticed that golfers were, if anything, more prone than even trial lawyers to complain about things going wrong through no fault of their own.

Damnit, by hindsight—not for the first time—Willis wished he had taken up a simpler line of work involving less exposure to "rub of the green", such as flying a spaceship.

CHAPTER 10

With shade thrown by the kid hovering over him like…shade, Max drove the *Cafenero* into the countryside northwest of town. Dumbo was counting on him to come up with a book that would draw attention to Yours Truly's good works and launch their publishing venture, but *Case of a Dangerous Old Lady*…

Max himself had to admit, to himself, that Mike Hammer, Sam Spade, Phillip Marlowe, no doubt Brad Runyon, and all the other famous gumshoes of *Noir* lore had steered clear of penny-ante investigations related to divorce, lost dogs and routine insurance claims. Also, he had to admit that reckless driving by little old Lady Booth-Montjoy looked to be not seriously criminal. In a nutshell, his investigation just didn't have the stuffings—even spiced up with adjectives provided by that James Patterson character—for a gripping *Maximo Morgan Mystery* that would make Yours Truly rich and famous.

If only the little old Lady's rear-ending of Dumbo's little car had been at least attempted murrrderrr. Or if the misdemeanor had been committed to further a second misdemeanor and the two offenses could be added up to a felony such as they charged Trump with, *Case of Dangerous Old Lady* would be a different story. Heck, Lady Booth-Montjoy was also rich, and famous in a way.

According to old newspaper articles, the Lady—once a plain ol' Miss Sybil Simpson—was the daughter of a big wheel who came down from Pennsylvania to manage a local plate glass company owned by his family. Sent off to Europe to be a debutante and get married, she had tied and untied knots with multiple mates—all named a Prince, a Duke, or a Lord—and a few years ago returned to family land outside of town to provide a natural home for animals a deceased husband had left to her. Rumor and gossip had it that the collection of foreign wildlife was responsible for scaring off the county's coyote population and song birds.

After arriving at the Lady's estate identified by sign as *Cross Brook Farm* and steering the *Cafenero* between two brick pedestals onto a long gravel driveway, sure enough, Max saw that grassy fields were decorated with a pack of stuffed dogs that looked to be running from a stuffed horse, which seemed to be carrying a red-coated rider. Then a large red brick mansion rose up at the end of the driveway, where he was barely able to squeeze the *Cafenero* under a carport.

Getting out of the vehicle's barrel seat proved to be also a dicey proposition, not to mention climbing down onto the gravel driveway. After brushing himself off, he ankled to a massive front door and strained to lift a large brass knocker for a single loud knock. Having never been at a Lady's mansion before, he expected to be met by a butler, but…bingo.

"Deliveries are to be made 'round back," said the little old Lady herself…up in years, but with bright red hair… standing in the doorway with a cat clutched in her arms… peering at him through thick rimless eyeglasses…

"Maximo Morgan, my Lady," said Max, with a tip of his fedora and attempted curtsy. "I'm investigating yesterday's unfortunate automotive mishap on Main Street, and would like to ask you a few questions about…"

"Oh dear, did that little man in that toy car succumb to his injuries?" she asked in what sounded like one of those high-class British accents. "What a pity. If you've come to take the unruly vehicle to jail, I'm afraid you have wasted the trip. The Rolls is in a shop, having its bonnet mended."

"The other driver is alive, but…"

"Well then, Constable, don't let me keep you from your more important duties."

Max clarified that he was a private dick, and had no important duties. He simply needed to ask a few questions for, uh, insurance purposes, he fibbed, but…

"I shan't involve insurance companies, Mr. Dick. The collision of vehicles was not my fault."

Aha, the plot got thicker.

Max took a small notebook and pen from a chest pocket of his jacket and prepared to jot another chapter in the same old story heard by every hawkshaw from Hoboken to Henryetta a hundred times before, a story titled "The Butler Did It". But he himself had witnessed Lady Booth-Montjoy's reckless rear-ending and already knew…

"Lord Byron was clawing at me, howling for attention and…"

"Lord Byron?"

"My cat. High speed makes him nervous and…"

"High speed?"

The obviously addled little old Lady—a neglected price tag dangled from an underarm of her obviously brand new peach-colored dress—went on to further incriminate herself by admitting that she'd had perhaps "one too many" drops of sherry at breakfast.

Dang it, according to the kid, mystery about who done it was important to making books gripping, but…Dang it, *Case of a Dangerous Old Lady* was turning out to be simpler than a ham sandwich without mustard.

Hmmm.

On the other hand, stories laced with so-called "human interest"…Max began to feel sorry for Lady Booth-Montjoy, and for himself. Helping Dumbo make local streets safe for kids at a little old Lady's expense would be like stealing candy from an underprivileged kid, but potentially what they called "heart warming".

And this particular little old Lady was loaded, he reminded himself. She could well afford…

"As long as you're here, Detective Dick, may I prevail upon you to assist me in a small matter?" she said, dropping Lord Byron to the ground and taking a slip of paper from a handbag strapped to a shoulder. "But no," she then said, "I suppose the local bank would not accept from a third party this check drawn on a London account. Oh dear, how is cook to stock the cupboard?"

Max readily agreed to haul the distressed little old Lady into town, but…

"Oh no, but God bless you," she said. "I'm still too shaken by yesterday's mishap to undertake the journey. Would you happen to have any food for cook's underprivileged children in your taco taxi?"

He had not yet stocked the *Cafenero* cupboard, but…What the heck, if Dumbo could rescue troubled youths somewhat off streets and Jerry Lewis could break legs for crippled children, a cash loan to feed underprivileged kids was the least a high roller such as himself could do.

After handing over a wad of Jeffersons and starting to take his leave, Max remembered to ask Lady Booth-Montjoy about the so-called "Flying Lady" a/k/a "Spirit of Ecstasy" hood ornament curiously missing from the Rolls

"In the wind!" she barked. "But don't look at me. Sure and it's the chauffeur's job to look after the mechanics of transportation."

Hmmm? To Max's ear, the little old Lady's accent seemed to have taken on a slightly Irish lilt.

WEDNESDAY

September 10, 2025

CHAPTER 11

As instructed by a Willis V. Willis call last night, Max again brought the *Cafenero* to a halt under the carport of Lady Booth-Montjoy's mansion. Again he tumbled from the vehicle. Again he dusted off himself, and after again knocking on the mansion's front door…

Hmmm.

He had a hunch the wobbly and somewhat disheveled little old Lady might have had more than one too many drops of sherry at breakfast. Though she was skinny as a stick of spaghetti, getting her into the *Cafenero* took some doing. After belting her into the shotgun barrel seat and firing up the horses under the hood of his new slightly used wheels…

"Hawkshaws and hounds: except for tails, just alike," she said with a noticeably Irish accent, dreamily gazing out into the estate's display of stuffed dogs, horse, and a lone rider chasing a fox. "Growing up in the countryside west of Philadelphia, my sisters and I used to rise at the crack of dawn to drag smoked kippers across surrounding fields."

Smoked kippers?

"Red herring, to you. What fun it was to divert the muckety-mucks on their high horses from tearing through Mother's cabbage patch like lords of the manor. And through the years since then…what fun."

Before he was able to freshen her memory about Monday's rear-ending on Main Street, the reckless driver nodded off and began to quietly snore.

Hmmm. It now struck Max as somehow odd that the little

old Lady herself, and not a chauffeur she'd mentioned, would have been at the wheel of the Rolls, but…

Oh well, arrived thirty minutes later at the Okmulgee County Courthouse, he gently roused Lady Booth-Montjoy from her nap. Ankling into the courthouse with her on his arm, he explained that his private dickwork for Dumbo Dumphy's lawsuit against her was not personal. He was just doing his P.I. duty, helping to hold her accountable for reckless driving in order to make streets safe for kids. Dumbo and he were not in it for the money.

In the same friendly manner, a smiling Willis V. Willis bounded across the courthouse lobby with an extended paw.

"So good of you to come on such short notice, Milady," the lawyer said, smooching her hand. "The quicker we get the Who-Struck-John out of the way, the sooner you can go about your leisure while I rassle with Lone Star Insurance Company."

"No need to have those nitpicking so-and-sos sticking their noses in," Lady Booth-Montjoy barked. "I settle traffic tickets out of my own pocket and keep my record clean."

Ankling down a courthouse hallway, Max noted that assignment of the case to old Judge Dwight was a lucky break. During a private session in the judge's chambers following a prior courtroom appearance as a witness, His Honor had compared him to a figurine of Lady Justice that sat on his desk: blindfolded, so to speak, not swayed by facts when weighing the pros and cons of cases and not…

"If called on by the judge, be brief and to the point," said Willis V. Willis as they entered the courtroom ringed by other lawyers standing in back and side aisles. "Judge Dwight doesn't suffer longwinded fools, and no doubt has a noonish tee-time scheduled."

"All rise!" a bailiff bellowed as His Honor entered, fluffed his black robe and took a seat behind his elevated desk. "Court is now in session, with the Honorable Timothy Dwight presiding. First on the docket: In the *Case of Clark Dumphy vs. Lady Booth-Montjoy*, plaintiff moves for Summary Judgement."

"Your Honor, this is an open-and-shut case involving no

dispute of relevant facts," said Willis V. Willis, after ankling into what was called a well and standing beside a table where Dumbo already sat — in a wheelchair and wearing a neck brace — smiling and looking full of confidence as usual. "At approximately 10 a.m on the morning of Monday, October…"

"Offer of proof?" said the judge, glancing at his watch.

"Yes, Your Honor, an eye-witness to the automotive rear-ending of my client has submitted a sworn statement, and is here today to testify if necessary…"

"Bring the witness forward," said Judge Dwight looking into the audience, and as Max stepped into a center aisle…"Oh no," said His Honor, slapping a hand to his forehead, obviously remembering he had forgotten something.

Max ankled into the well and — reminded by Willis V. Willis to be brief — swore to tell the truth and said:

"Mr. Dumphy and Yours Truly had an important meeting scheduled to discuss a big deal. You see, Judge Dwight, thousands if not millions of manhole covers go missing every year and our joint venture intends to…"

"Get to the point, Morgan!"

"Well, you see, almost all manhole covers are round and easy to roll by thieves who have no regard for law and…"

"Just tell what you saw with your 'private eye' that bears on this case, and be quick about it!"

Without interesting background and gripping adjectives, Max told that he had been standing at a Main Street curb in downtown Henryetta, waiting to be picked up by Dumbo, whose little car got stuck in a wrong lane. After circling the block, but again getting in the wrong traffic lane, Dumbo had weaved into the right-hand lane and stopped. A speeding red Rolls-Royce then crashed into the rear of the little Cooper MINI. Someone must have immediately called the police, because within seconds a black-and-white raced to the scene of the accident, but for some reason sped by without noticing that Mr. Dumphy had been whiplashed.

"Yours Truly helped the victim into my nearby office, where

we discussed the details for our big deal while waiting for a Doc on Wheels to arrive. You see, no matter what Encyclopedia Brown says, square manhole covers will…"

"Enough! I have only a few minutes to hear what counsel for the Defendant has to say."

"I don't need no pettyfogger," said Lady Booth-Montjoy, staggering also into the well. "I already told this hawkshaw what happened, and it was not my fault."

The little old Lady nevertheless then stated that the chauffeur was "sleeping it off" Monday morning, and that while traveling at "nerve wracking speed" she had been distracted by her cat, Lord Byron, when "the Rolls bumped into little Dumbo…I mean crashed into the little car occupied by Mr. Dumphy. It's that unruly foreign automobile with the awkward steering wheel that's at fault," she concluded. "Not me."

Little Dumbo? Yeah, his client and partner was of sawed-off physical stature, but for Lady Booth-Montjoy to almost affectionately call him "little", and by nickname…

"Well, I suppose I will have to hear a few words about the Plaintiff's alleged injuries before making a ruling," the judge said, after again putting a hand to his forehead.

Striding into the well, "Good morning, Two Putt, uh, I mean Your Honor," said Dr. Mettenbaugh, the Doc on Wheels who had come to Dumbo's aid. "I was on wheels day before yesterday and responded to a 10-50-with-PI call. By the time I got to the scene of the accident involving personal injury, Mr. Dumphy had been moved into a nearby copy shop cubicle, complaining of neck pain consistent with a cervical acceleration-deceleration injury commonly referred to by common laymen as injury resulting from 'whiplash'."

Obviously moved to sympathy for Dumbo and "there-but-for-the-grace-of-God" concern for himself, Judge Dwight looked up to the ceiling and muttered: "Spare me, Lord."

"After transferring the patient to our clinic on wheels and obtaining x-rays, I confirmed my initial diagnosis that a blow from the rear had compressed the thoracic spine, causing the cervical spine to deform into an S-shape where the lower cervical spine maintains its lordosis. Accordingly, I sold a neck brace to Mr. Dumphy, administered aspirin and gave him Mr. Willis' card. In my expert professional opinion, the patient will have to wear the neck brace for the rest of his life, and will never be able to fully recover his bearings by swiveling his head."

Pathetically but bravely, Dumbo faintly smiled straight into space.

"Okay, that's it then," said Judge Dwight, raising his gavel, but...

"Hold that thought!" a woman's voice loudly shrieked.

Max wheeled around and saw a youngish redheaded dame rushing from the gallery into the well toward the judge, waving a sheaf of papers, shouting: "I move to intervene in this case on behalf of my client, namely Rhonda Pickens Dumphy, soon to be ex-spouse of the Plaintiff, Clark Dumphy!"

And...Oh no, seeing Dumbo swivel his head, Max had an uneasy feeling of wheels coming off *Case of A Dangerous Old Lady*.

CHAPTER 12

Following her feisty lawyer to the front of the courtroom with a bulky satchel clutched in her arms, Rhonda could see that the judge was not receptive to Clarise's attempt to "intervene" in Dumbo's personal injury lawsuit. Also looking none too happy was her husband's jowly lawyer. But Dumbo himself…

"On what grounds do you dare to barge into my courtroom and make such a 'Motion'," the judge growled. "Bailiff…"

"The Motion is based on my contention that any judgement awarded to the Plaintiff in this matter will constitute a marital asset, which his wife of more than twenty years is entitled to share in event of divorce, for which she has filed within the past hour."

"I object, Your Honor!" the jowly lawyer bellowed. "Divorce and splitting up marital pots-and-pans are matters entirely separate from the matter currently before the Court and…A divorce action against my client is no doubt a can of worms that should be kicked down the road."

"Mr. Willis is right, Ms. What's-Your-Name," the judge barked at Clarise. "I don't have time to hear your Motion even if I had a mind to. I'm due at…Your client's Divorce Petition will have to be handled in due course by…"

"My name is Clarise Kilpatrick. I am a duly licensed attorney. And with due respect, Your Honor, I know Clark Dumphy and, by reputation, Mr. Willis V. Willis, to be dilatory in the extreme. Delay here and now will result in endless delay later for countless Motions and ongoing tedious process, during which time marital assets under Mr. Dumphy's control—specifically including a favorable judgement in this lawsuit—are sure to be hidden if not wasted."

"Sorry, Ms. Kilpatrick, you will have to address those issues with another judge at another time. I myself am already running late for urgent…"

"My client's Petition for Divorce has been assigned to you, Judge Dwight. Unless you kill two birds today, it is you who will be endlessly besieged by Mr. Dumphy's lawyer from Vulture Row."

"Assigned to me?! Damn that Clerk. She uses me like a rented mule, and a redheaded one at that. No offense intended, Ms. Kilpatrick."

"None taken, Your Honor. My client and I have come prepared to lessen your load."

"Under no circumstances will I be representing Mr. Dumphy in a divorce case, here and now or ever!" Dumbo's lawyer shouted.

Rhonda clutched the satchel tighter. Her reluctance to divorce Dumbo had been based on fear of having to divulge her personal financial situation under oath. Her no-account husband—with the aid of a no-account lawyer and possibly a no-account judge—would no doubt claim that her substantial inheritance and earnings on its investment were marital assets, and half his. Though Clarise had convinced her she stood to net far more by intervening in Dumbo's personal injury lawsuit and staking her claim to monetary damages while she could, the very thought of him reciprocally getting a share of her own nest egg was galling.

Nevertheless…Seeing as how the lawsuit seemed to have gone in Dumbo's favor, Rhonda—with a sigh—surrendered the satchel into her lawyer's outstretched hands.

As Clarise opened the stash of financial records and began handing copies to the judge and Dumbo's lawyer, Rhonda felt a slight pang of pity. Clark Dumphy was a natural-born con man, like his father before him. In high school, without athletic ability or good looks for chasing girls with any hope of scoring, his sport had been to show-off cleverness by beating "the system", not so much for the small change he picked up, but for the sake of winning "the game." And since then, most if not all of his marks had been as much as accomplices to his petty cons. No one got killed, and…

Truth be told, her tricky husband and she were not unalike. She herself…

"As you can clearly see, Your Honor, Mrs. Dumphy inherited a substantial sum from her mother," Clarise was saying, "and thereafter made a point to keep her personal financial affairs secretly separate and apart from marital affairs."

After returning to the courtroom seating area and collapsing into a pew, Rhonda vividly recalled watching an old movie on tv with her grandpa when she was only ten or eleven. In the film titled *A Big Hand for the Little Lady*, the five richest men in a wild west territory had gathered at a saloon for an annual high-stakes poker game. Passing through town, a poor man and wife on their way to buying a farm were forced to delay their dream, due to their rickety old covered wagon breaking down. The husband—a lot like Dumbo, she later realized—got into the poker game, put the family's life savings into a pot, and collapsed at the table when the high rollers raised his bet to way more than he could match.

"What I clearly see in these bank account records is evidence of Mrs. Dumphy having strictly extra-marital affairs," the lawyer named Willis was saying, despite Dumbo pulling at the sleeve of his jacket. "What I see are deposits of proceeds from sales of her goods in the back alley of her own Easy Pickens Shop."

As co-owner of the poker hand her husband had been playing, the pioneer woman went to the local bank for help. The bank owner—an old man known to be tighter than a wet boot about lending money—came to the saloon, took a look at the poker hand, and agreed to put down five thousand dollars to keep her in the game. Having dealt with the old banker themselves and knowing his reputation for never putting money at risk, the high rollers folded their hands, the wife won a pot amounting to twenty thousand dollars, and afterward…Uh oh.

"No, it looks to me like Mrs. Dumphy has co-mingled her

inherited funds with those of this back alley co-venture with her husband," the judge was saying as he scanned her bank statements. "I see here, for instance, notation of her Mister's consignment of a Rolls-Royce hood ornament for sale in the Whatnot Shop she operates, and records of numerous other such co-mingling."

Rhonda sighed. In the old movie, it turned out that the husband and wife were grifters, secretly invited to town by the old banker, who had previously been swindled by the high rollers. The poker hand was in fact a loser, the bluff with his backing was a con, and now in her own "game" against Dumbo…

"It is the Court's judgement that funds put away by Mrs. Dumphy are sure enough marital assets, and that Mr. Dumphy is entitled to half."

"I object!" Dumbo's own lawyer nevertheless shouted. "This… This redheaded Counselette for Mrs. Dumphy is trying to horn in on my lawsuit through a back alley door and grab a share of fees rightfully due only to me upon settlement of damages through negotiation with Lone Star Insurance Company. It is solely myself…I mean, it is my client alone, not the Missus, who is suffering severe pain in the neck, doomed to never again to get his bearings!"

"I have no intention to involve that insurance company!" a little old lady in the audience shouted.

"Damages will come out of your pocket if not theirs!" the agitated lawyer shouted back. "We're looking at millions here, my Lady."

Though annoyed to have to share what was rightfully hers alone, bearing the insult was worth it for getting half of millions for Dumbo's injury, and for spite.

"Sauce for the gander, sauce for the goose, Mr. Dumphy," said the judge. "You've got to throw all that you have, or get, into the marital pot."

"Other than my share of what Rhonda stashed away, I am dead broke," said Dumbo, after struggling to his feet. "If not for those marital assets of hers, I wouldn't have a pot to pee in."

"Petition for Divorce granted. Fifty-fifty split of marital property ordered. Now let's move on to this Motion for Summary Judgement."

Hmmm.

If only because of the canary-eating smirk on Dumbo's face—possibly not faking brain damage—Rhonda had an uneasy feeling that her fast-talking "Lone Lawyer's" strategy of snatching half her ex's "roadkill" might have been somehow amiss, and that she herself may have bet on a losing hand dealt to her in a possibly rigged game.

CHAPTER 13

Not a pot to pee in?!

Max was dumbfounded by Dumbo Dumphy's statement to the judge. How could the successful wheeler-dealer be "dead broke"? Only two days ago Yours Truly had handed over, or rather had invested most of his life savings in Dumphy's square manhole cover venture. Now the high roller was claiming…Had Yours Truly been played for a sucker?

After barely curbing an urge to charge back into the well and frisk his business partner, Max got a grip on himself.

He was nobody's fool, he reminded himself. He had been around the block a few times. He knew the score. Heck, Judge Dwight had already ruled that Dumbo was entitled to half the boatload of clams his soon-to-be ex-wife had salted away. And from what the judge had also said—thanks to Yours Truly's eye-witness account of Dumbo's lucky accident—it looked sure as money in the bank that his partner would be getting a judgement worth millions for his personal injury.

Even though the *Case of a Dangerous Old Lady* might not have the makings for a gripping mystery involving crime, his investment in Dumbo's other venture still looked to be solid as Plymouth Rocks.

As the judge raised a hand to bring down the hammer on a happy ending…

Boom! came a sound of distant thunder, and…

"Arrest that woman!" someone shouted. "She is a serial shoplifter!'

What in Sam Hill? Down the center aisle and into the well

went a semi-familiar frizzy-haired blonde, followed by the Henryetta Chief of Police, a do-nutter named Potter. The het up broad swiveled and pointed a long bright red fingernail into the audience at…Lady Booth-Montjoy?

Boom! Boom!

"Sorry for the interruption, Judge," said Potter, "but I had to bring my wife to Okmulgee for a medical appointment, and like you always say: justice delayed is justice denied."

"You brought your wife to my courtroom for medical treatment?! Bailiff…"

"No, Your Honor. Here with me is Ms. Lulu LeBelle, owner of *Fresh Fashions Marche* in my town of Henryetta, and…"

"That old woman came into my *Marche* two days ago, and this time I caught on to her scam!"

"Objection, Your Honor!" said Willis V. Willis, again up on his feet and redder in the face than ever. "This…This accusation has no bearing on the matter at hand, and time for your scheduled, uh, recess, is near."

As Lady Booth-Montjoy just sat there beside him, sniffing into a handkerchief, Max smelled another case of gross police incompetence. Or…Hmmm, had the little old lady sneaked in smoked kippers for a snack?

Boom! Boom!

Following sounds of closer rolling thunder, Judge Dwight looked at his watch, sighed, and…"In view of the storm coming in, I will hear the charges impeaching the credibility of the Defendant," His Honor announced.

Boom! Boom!

"That fingersmith sitting there came in like always, wearing a shabby housedress," Ms. LeBelle ranted. "I took my eye off her to ring up a sale, but glanced up and noticed she had changed into one of my frocks—a stylish peach-colored one—and was hurrying out the door. I called the cops, then went to the front and saw her get into that fancy red car of hers. She just sat there, like she was waiting for someone to come by, then took off when she heard the police car sirens."

"I got tired of waiting while you tended to that rich bitch," the little old Lady said in a calm little old ladylike manner.

Max edged closer and took her hand to show moral support.

Boom! Boom!

"We tracked down Lady Booth-Montjoy's red Rolls to Rocco's Body Shop & Auto Salvage" said Potter, a *faux* Five-O if there ever was one. "In the trunk, we found a bunch of ordinary used dresses, and a stash of new high-fashion merchandise, with price tags from stores here in Okmulgee still attached!"

"For crying out loud, Judge," said Willis V. Willis. "Obviously, there's been a minor mix-up, hardly deserving of a police raid on your courtroom to bust a little old lady for allegedly…"

Boom! Boom!

While remaining physically seated beside the little old Lady, in spirit Max stood four-square behind Willis V. Willis versus Pete Potter, a smalltime Barney Fife armed with a badge, but otherwise clueless about crime detection. On a Halloween in the recent past, the uniformed flatfoot had fallen for a dame's disappearing act, and came within a whisker of charging both her husband and a high school boyfriend with murrrderrr. Thanks to private dicking by Yours Truly…

Boom! Boom! Boom!

"To clear the air of a distracting odor, the Court will be in recess for fifteen minutes," the Judge declared with a bang of his gavel. "Upon my return to the bench, I will dispose of this entire kettle of kippers."

BOOM!

CHAPTER 14

The thunderstorm had passed, but in the still muggy air Willis sensed the supreme law of the land weighing down on what should have been a simple Motion for Summary Judgement in the cut-and-dried *Case of Clark Dumphy vs. Lady Booth-Montjoy.* That would be not the U.S. Constitution tipping the scales of justice, but Murphy's Law, under which anything that could go wrong would go wrong at the worst possible time.

Damnit, the judge's ruling that damages obtained for his client's personal injury would be a marital asset—making the unsettled claim half-owned by the greedy Missus—had put his full fee in jeopardy. At the very least, future litigious argle-bargle versus the wife's feisty redheaded lawyer was now in the offing. In other words, despite his firm policy to get paid for his pettyfogging, to protect his prospective fee for handling Dumphy's personal injury claim he'd been forced to become involved in the Dumphy couple's divorce case!

And in addition to that revolting reversal of fortune, now found himself in the odd position of having to defend - without an additional fee—the Defendant he was suing, against criminal charges of petty shoplifting. Otherwise, when the time came to negotiate a settlement of damages, the Lone Star Insurance Company's cagy lawyer, Big Game Bob Huckaby, would no doubt claim that Lady Booth-Montjoy's liability coverage did not extend to her use of the Rolls-Royce for dangerous criminal purposes.

Putting his fee further in jeopardy, if forced to look to the Defendant herself, he would no doubt find that her wealth was inherited and wrapped in an iron-clad trust.

Put simply, the bird's nest on the ground was looking—and smelling—more like a cow pie that he was being forced to…

Now the judge was returning from his chambers, likely having re-set a tee time. Hopefully, "Two-Putt" Dwight would now be even more eager than usual to cut through tedious legal process and dispose of…

"All rise. The Court is back in session, the Honorable Timothy Dwight presiding. Presently pending: Motion for Summary Judgement by Plaintiff in *Case of*…"

"Let's first get back to what the Defendant was doing at the time of the accident alleged to have caused Plaintiff's personal injury," said the judge. "If you have something to say on this issue, Counselor, spout it with minimum wind."

Forced to roll with the punches, so to speak, Willis addressed the cop:

"Chief Potter, would you please briefly walk the court through the investigation that led you to suspect Lady Booth-Montjoy is guilty of shoplifting clothes from the store called *Fresh Fashions Marche*."

"It was no brief walk-through a park, I can tell you that. We've had reports of shoplifting from Ms. LeBelle before, and other reports of similar thefts in surrounding towns that mentioned a red getaway vehicle. When Ms. LeBelle called in a 10-35 Monday morning—that's police code for major crime alert—my top deputy set out in hot pursuit, but…"

"But what? Did your deputy, in reckless hot pursuit of an unidentified citizen, force a randomly encountered red car to collide with my client's vehicle? Based on a so-called '10-35 call' made by an hysterical shop owner, did you cuff a little old lady, drag her to jail, and use a rubber hose to…"

"Defund the police!" Mrs. Dumphy's lawyer shrieked.

"Shoplifting is not bargain shopping!" Ms. LeBelle shouted.

"Order in the Court!" His Honor declared.

"Well, no, we were unable to do any of that," said the Chief. "Following standard procedures, it took us a while to dope out that the perp had staged a rear-ender on Main Street as a diversion to avoid apprehension. The dirty trick backfired when my deputy stepped into a puddle of antifreeze in the street, indicating the collision had punctured her car's radiator. We tracked the damaged vehicle to Rocco's Body Shop late yesterday, searched the trunk and…"

Uh oh. Willis paused in hopes of hearing another distracting outburst from Mrs. Dumphy's redheaded lawyer, followed by the bang of Judge Dwight's gavel, but…crickets.

"You searched the trunk legally as authorized by a warrant signed by Judge Dwight, I assume."

"Leave me out of this, Counselor!" the old judge roared.

"Well, Judge Dwight was still out on a golf course and had left strict orders…Dang it, we were in hot pursuit of a shoplifter on the loose!"

"Defund the Police!"

"Shoplifting is not shopping!"

"Order in the Court!"

"Searched the trunk late yesterday, you say, still in 'hot pursuit' thirty hours after giving chase?" Willis continued.

"No Justice. No Peace!"

"No tickee. No 'laundry'!"

"Order! Order in the Court!"

"Well…" said the Chief of Police, scratching his head.

"Your Honor, I move that the charges against Lady Booth-Montjoy be dismissed, and…"

"I second the emotion!" the redheaded female mouthpiece shrieked.

"Throw the book at her!" Ms. Lulu LeBelle demanded.

"I further request that we proceed with my Motion for…"

"Request granted!" said the judge with a bang of his gavel. "Next time, Chief Potter, slow down your hot pursuit of little old ladies and don't be so het up to pinch them."

Willis heaved a sigh of relief.

"Now that we've played through that bottleneck, let's move on," said the judge. "In the *Case of Clark Dumphy vs. Lady Booth-*

Montjoy, plaintiff's Motion for Summary Judgement is hereby…"

"Stop the music!" someone shouted. "There's a crooked game of Three-Card Monte going on here!"

Willis turned his head…saw a portly middle-aged man—an agent for 'Mr. Murphy', so to speak—hurrying toward the judge's bench…heard him holler that he was in fact an agent for Lone Star Insurance Company and that a con game was afoot.

With a sigh of resignation, Willis slumped into his chair at the table beside his official client, Clark Dumphy, who continued to just sit there, still grinning at his estranged Missus like a bullfrog squatting in a slaughterhouse feed lot full of flies.

CHAPTER 15

Con game afoot? No way, José.

Max saw through the charge for what it really was: showboating by a loudmouthed politician, namely Buford Bailey, longtime Mayor of Henryetta and proprietor of an also longtime family-owned insurance agency.

After losing the most recent mayoral election, Bailey had ranted long and hard that the ballpoint pens used by voters to mark ballots had been hacked. Faced with threat of a lawsuit, the winning candidate let Bailey have the thankless unpaid job, and national news media lost interest in the clown. No doubt hoping to get back into a spotlight…

"I happen to know that Lady Booth-Montjoy is currently on a grand tour of a foreign continent," Bailey bellowed. "That old woman sitting there, bold as brass, is the Lady's housemaid, Mary Margaret Doyle a/k/a Mary Margaret McGuffin!"

Ohhhhh, lawyers standing in the aisles ohhhhhed.

Max took his hand from the hand of…

"I never said I was no one except meself!" the…the old woman sitting beside him hollered.

Ohhhhh…

"Ms. Doyle…"

"I operate under me maiden name as a proud McGuffin!"

"… is a notorious bunco artist from Pennsylvania, with a record as long as my arm," Bailey continued, with a stubby finger pointed at the old maiden.

Ohhhhh…

Max scooted away from the…the suspect, now slouched in a

somewhat unladylike manner, with her legs apart.

"I object to this eleventh-hour sideshow!" Willis V. Willis shouted.

"Ditto my colleague's objection!" Mrs. Dumphy's lawyer shrieked.

"I told you she is a common fingersmith!" Ms. LeBelle hollered.

Ohhhhh…

"Order in the Court!" the judge declared, banging his gavel. "Order…"

Max had a feeling he would be rolling in clover alright, but six feet under, and…

"Your Honor, in case this false accusation happens to be, uh, factual—contrary to my professional investigator's assurances—I hereby amend my petition and name Ms. Doyle a/k/a McGuffin as a co-defendant in my client's personal injury lawsuit," said Willis. "For liability and insurance purposes, she—a trusted member of Lady Booth-Montjoy's household—would be expected to be an occasional driver of the Rolls-Royce that crashed into my client's rear end."

Max heaved a sigh of relieve, but…

"Absolutely not!" Bailey declared. "Lady Booth-Montjoy is both generous and, uh, frugal. She takes down-and-outers such as this matchstick mama into her service as acts of charity, but never trusts them. Her Lone Star Insurance Company policy—that I myself wrote up—specifically lists only herself and her chauffeur as authorized drivers of her vehicle."

Ohhhhh…

"Irrelevant!" Willis howled. "Liability attaches to the insured vehicle like, uh, like a hood ornament!"

"Yes, like a Flying Lady in this case," the redheaded female lawyer added.

Ha, Ha, Ha, Ha, Ha…

"That flimflam floozie no doubt heisted my Lady's Spirit of Ecstasy!" Bailey blustered. "The chauffeur filed a claim."

Ha, Ha, Ha, Ha, Ha…

As onlookers rolled in the aisles, so to speak, Max began to suspect the crafty old broad had in fact conned Dumbo, but…

"The plaintiff in this case, Mr. Clark Dumphy, is also an incorrigible bunco artist," said Bailey, pointing another stubby finger. "He himself has filed at least seven fraudulent claims in the past, also based on 'swoop-and-squat' maneuvers in which he purposely exposes himself to rear-ending by suddenly stopping after swerving in front of other vehicles. Docs on Wheels across the state have 'diagnosed' his 'whiplash injuries' on multiple occasions."

Ohhhhh…

His new business partner had likely only had a run of bad luck, Max hoped. Heck, nobody could change lanes in a mini-car without sometimes getting rear-ended. People who didn't really know Dumbo must have mistook his occasional misfortune for…

"I take back my rash request for divorce!" Mrs. Dumphy screeched, rushing from the gallery into the well. "I renew my marriage vow for richer or poorer," she declared as she frantically scooped up her financial records from a table.

Ohhhhh…

To judge by the tears running down her cheeks, Max could tell the dame was on the level, but…

"Too late, Easy," said Dumbo, smiling, and—to Max's relief—seeming still confident he would win the personal injury case and get paid off for whiplash. But Willis V. Willis…

"Your Honor, as unwitting attorney for Mr. Dumphy in this matter," said the famous litigator, also moved to tears, "I have spent countless hours on his behalf, for which—given that Mr. Dumphy won rights to half the marital assets previously held secretly by his wife—I request that Your Honor order payment of fees and reimbursement of costs in an amount of not less than…"

"The Court hereby orders that costs of litigation of these matters be paid to the Clerk by Counsel, in compensation for interference in my regular…for waste of the Court's time based on careless 'investigation' bordering on attorney malpractice.

Case of Clark Dumphy vs. Lady Booth-Montjoy et al is hereby dismissed!"

Ohhhhh…

The phony little old Lady seemed to have flown the coop, but as Dumbo wheeled from the well beside his ex-Missus…

"I knew better than to file for divorce against you, Easy," Max heard Dumbo say. "You would have fibbed about what you had stashed away. But I also knew you would never voluntarily take the risk of getting caught telling lies under oath by divorcing me unless you thought I had hit a jackpot. So to get what is legally half mine…"

"Get over yourself, Dumbo. You were dumb-lucky to stumble into the marital-asset score as a consolation prize. For you to have staged The Flop in the path of another grifter without insurance or a pot to pee in, what a chump! Ha, Ha, Ha."

"The laugh's on you, Easy," Max then heard Dumbo say, as he followed his partner and the ex-wife into the courthouse hallway. "Mary Margaret was fencing the Rolls hood ornament. I scored the Flying Lady for your birthday. We got to talking about marriage partners not keeping vows and…"

"Yeah, you would know that line of 'for richer or poorer'."

"You and your also greedy lawyer fell for the bait-and-switch, Easy. It was a classic Kansas City Shuffle from the git-go: One, you suspected a con, my flop. Two, distracted, you tried to buy into the game. Three, you were wrong about the real scam. Admit it, Hon: I pulled off a long con."

Yeah, like the savvy Captain Trumble put it back in the *Noir*: the bunco artist, the swindler, the con man came in a thousand disguises, with a million tricks up his sleeve, Max recalled the kid warning. And as someone else had doped out: there was a sucker born every…Heck, for a minute, or two, even Yours Truly thought he might have put down money in a game and lost all his marbles.

But not every flimflam came to an unhappy ending, Max was happy to note. From the con pulled on his shifty Missus, Dumbo now had his mitts on big bucks that—in Yours Truly's

book—his partner had coming. So their unrollable manhole covers venture was still on, and —even without anyone getting bumped off in *Case of a Dangerous Old Lady*—the publishing venture with the artful wheeler-dealer still had…wheels.
THE
END

GENERATION GAPS

A Maximo Morgan Mystery

OCTOBER

WILLIAM LEROY

ISBN 979-8-9869494-8-2
$7.99
50799>
9 798986 949482
MP
Mossik Press
GENERATION GAPS
OCTOBER
FIGHT
FIGHT FOR YOUTH IN ASIA!
WILLIAM LEROY

TUESDAY

October 14, 2025

♫Well the generation gap is a mighty big hole/

You ain't gonna fill it with all the lies bein' told/

Wah Wah Wah Wah you'd better clean your house/

If you expect to narrow the generation gap/

Wah Wah Wah Wah Wah Wah Wah Wah Wah…♫

Betty Craig, Charlie Craig, Jim Hayner

CHAPTER ONE

At his desk inside the Mister Quickie copy shop workstation cubicle that served as his office, Max swiveled his double-wide chair forty-five degrees to the left… back to center… forty-five degrees to the right… back to center… forty-five degrees to the left…back to center…

Phew! The sittercise routine was exhausting, but… "Don't stop!" Roberta Peters barked from across the desk. "We've got to shed fifty pounds of baby fat to get you in shape for marching."

He had started keeping social company with Roberta following kicks of buckets by both her mother and sister back in February…regularly watching tv together on the sofa inside the house he'd always shared with his mom…and lately, at Mom's insistence, regularly enjoying "popcorn-and-Netflix"—as the younger generation would put it—on a love seat inside the house Roberta had always shared with her late mom. Their common interest was doping out documentaries of private dickwork cases handled by famous gumshoes dating back to the *Noir*. But…

"No pain, no gain, Max!".

Two weeks ago Roberta—a nurse at the local hospital's Emergency Ward—had switched from the graveyard shift to working four-to-midnight, which had interrupted their once-a-week evening routine, and led to her moving in with him. To be a sort of a "sounding board" not unlike Arthur Hastings was for Hercule Poirot had been the idea. But in practice—more like Tuppence Beresford, the nitpicking wife and partner of Tommy Beresford in cases also reported by Agatha Christie—his cubicle mate had interrupted Yours Truly's daily routine by putting the

kibosh on snacks and…

"Sweat beats suet, Max. Pick up the pace!"

…forty-five degrees to the left…back to center…forty-five degrees to the right…back to center…forty-two or three degrees to the left…

"Pardon me for interrupting," said a trembling female voice. "Are you still the private detective known as the Fat Man?"

Swiveled back to center, Max opened his peepers and saw that a semi-familiar elderly woman was seating herself in the client chair.

"Maximo Morgan's the name," he said. "And yeah, Yours Truly's role model was Brad Runyon, a savvy gumshoe from back in the *Noir* known by oldtime radio case reports as the original Fat Man. Overweight, but light on his feet, and a good dancer. Middle-aged but hip to the scene, and a natty dresser. Unflappable when caught in tight spots, with a knack for unraveling cases of…"

"Murder? Do you have a knack for unraveling cases of attempted murder?"

Max's ears perked up. He had crossed paths with the old woman before, but didn't recall…

"Why, you are Mineola Phlegming, the mother of my Emergency Ward nursing colleague," said Roberta, scooting her own chair closer to the walk-in client. "I've heard all about you and your other daughter, Claudette."

Claudette Phlegming? He'd had multiple run-ins with the prickly high school teacher.

"Tell us about the case of attempted murder that needs unravelling," said his sounding board.

"Well, I got a glimpse of a pillow coming down on my face. And my heart…my bladder…"

"Chest pains?…Uncontrolled urination?" said Max. "And bright white light filling your head, right?"

"No, all I saw was blackness before my other daughter, Penny, came in and saved me from Claudette's attempted matricide."

Matricide?

Heck, keeping an aged parent alive was a person's sacred duty. Yours Truly had lived with his own mom since birth. Roberta had done the same until her mom bought a farm and…The only documentary of mother murder that came to mind was *Case of Throw Momma From the Train.*

"I'm sure you must be mistaken, Minnie," said Roberta, putting an arm on the shoulders of the old woman who had dodged a…a pillow. "Max is not yet as 'light on his feet' as we would like, and as for his unravelling knack…Not to worry, dear, I myself will personally straighten out this…this misunderstanding."

Max bit his lip. Yeah, there was a "misunderstanding' likely in play alright. In *Case of Throw Momma From the Train* two losers hatched a plot for one to rub out the other mope's cranky aged momma in return for a murderous son knocking off his co-plotter's ex-wife. By scratching each other's back, neither would have a detectable motive for the crime they individually committed. Both wrong numbers would skate murder raps.

But in what Max mentally filed as *Case of a Broad With an Itch* an even more devious dodge looked to be afoot.

CHAPTER TWO

Claudette Phlegming stood next to a blackboard inside her high school classroom, looking upon a herd of so-called students, thirty of them staring back at her like uncomprehending goats penned on shag carpet and…. No, they were more like a passel of proverbial pigs to whom she was professionally obliged to cast pearls acquired by her many years of study—at great expense—in the ivory towers of academia.

She was a teacher. Her field was Herstory—enlightened feminist interpretation of events past, present and future—and her usual lesson plan was to stress the urgent need to destroy western civilization, but…

Today Claudette had more urgent personal concerns on her mind. And so—though her expertise was in Gender Studies and Critical Marxist Theory, not Mathematics—she turned to the blackboard and chalked:

$6,500,000,000,000!

"That is numerical code for the sum of six-and-a-half trillion dollars," she explained, "which happens to be the approximate amount of money the United States federal government spent last year—and will spend in every year to come—on such things as military personnel and equipment used to maintain American oppression of other peoples.

"Even more immorally, however, are the expenditures the government makes for the comfort and enjoyment of elderly American people living luxuriously in balmy climes such as Florida, the so-called elephants grave yard. Ha! Elephants, the most thoughtful of beasts, know when the decent thing to do is

wander off and die, not carry on at public expense for exclusively their own individual and social security to the annual tune of…"

$1,500,000,000,000!!

"But wait! There's more of other people's money spent every year on the unfair and futile attempt to maintain the lives of oldsters past a respectable expiration age of sixty-five!"

$850,000,000,000!!!

"Add up these two wasted expenditures on the elderly and what do you get?" Claudette rhetorically asked, as she chalked:

$6,500,00…

"Actually, the current annual outlays for Social Security and Medicare would add up to two trillion, three hundred and fifty billion dollars", said one of the class' two smarty-pants brats, Orville Bennett.

"I was rounding up," said Claudette, "to… to reflect the fact that these 'outlays' are annual, uh, bound to increase, and to compare them to this measly number!"

$1,600,000,000,000!!!!

"Which happens to be the approximate total amount of the federal government student loans currently outstanding, a paltry sum that Biden promised to cancel with what would have been a small step for a shuffling old man, but a giant leap for humankind, specifically including me!"

Oh the pigs grunted in unison.

"Instead, the drooling old man dribbled out less than $200 billion by executive orders replete with catches such as requirements that I engage in public service or prove my disabilities."

Oh.

Claudette ranted on to further explain that due to usurious interest charges on unpaid balances of student loans, many if not most well educated academics such as herself were now trapped in amounts of debt exceeding what they had borrowed! Twenty-five percent of all victims were members of Black families, sixty-six percent were women, ten percent were holders of graduate degrees, many enslaved by debt in excess of $100,000… unable

to get home mortgage loans…unable to continue with advanced studies…even subject to having their meager salaries garnished after ten years on non-payment!

"My father paid off his tech school loans, bought a house, and set up a savings account for me and my sister to go to college," said the class' second smartass, Henry Rundell.

"Goody for your sugar daddy, a plumber, I believe. I on the other cleaner hand am an activist academic—holder of four Masters Degrees—dedicated to working for social and personal justice from inside the ivory tower. While I would not compare my efforts to unclogging pipes, I would say that… Well, it is difficult to judge which is the greater injustice: old fat cats being paid Social Security benefits on a par near to a high school teacher's salary—for playing golf, strolling on beaches and attending daily cocktail parties—or to keep them alive by Medicare at my expense!"

Oh.

Claudette lectured that whereas the average outstanding student loan balance was approximately $40,000, almost four times that amount was being paid by Medicare for individuals over sixty-five, including $50,000 during the last useless year of life, and over $20,000 during the last month! Nursing homes and other old-fossil warehousing facilities were chock full of virtual zombies… lying in bed…staring blankly at silent tv screens… being fed soft delicacies such as *fois gras*, to judge by the tab.

"Over seven million are currently afflicted with Alzheimer's and related dementia, with life expectancies of five-to-ten years. So do the math. At a Medicare cost of, say, $50,000 a year…"

"Hey, that's my grandpa you're talking about, Ms. Phlegming!"

Oh.

"Sorry about that, Mister Rogers. Nothing personal. I would say the same about my own mother. In the ongoing struggle for social justice, it's them or us."

Oh.

And in fact Claudette had long been thinking, if not exactly

saying in public, that her mother — Mineola a/k/a Minnie — was long past deserving social justice.

CHAPTER THREE

In both disguise and a sweat, Max drove his mom's brown Buick boiler west on Main Street toward the local high school. Though Roberta had interrupted his intended grilling of Old Lady Phlegming, he already had a book on the deadly daughter.

About eighteen months ago, he had crossed the Herstory teacher by resisting her effort to "transition" Yours Truly to female status.

About six months later, in his role as a Notary Public that paid the rent for his use of the Mister Quickie copy shop cubicle, he had balked at stamping a deed bearing the signature of a "Mineola Phlegming" that he'd not actually witnessed.

And just last January he had exposed the high school teacher and girls badminton team coach for loading up cafeteria food with tofu made of soybeans, a/k/a testosterone suppressors responsible for weakening legs and other body parts of boys on the rassling team.

In other words, yeah, Yours Truly was the guy in danger of being thrown off a train by the Phlegming broad's criminal cohort in return for her offing the old woman. And Suspect *Numero Uno* was a joker named Howard Taylor, the high school Principal.

During his most recent run-in with Claudette Phlegming—who worked under Taylor—he'd picked up a vibe of secret "coziness" between them. And yeah, in case after case from back in the *Noir* and since then, it was *femmes fatale* like the Phlegming broad who got dame-dizzy saps like Taylor to scratch their backs.

As for the question of what Taylor might have against Old Lady Phlegming that would drive him to put the daughter up to matricide…?

Arrived at the high school parking lot for visitors, Max adjusted the plastic nose with attached eyeglasses, black brows and mustache that disguised his true identity…got out of the boiler and…by chance, spotted the lookalike fat kid and wannabe P.I. who—prior to Roberta becoming Yours Truly's sounding board—had served as his case report jotter in the mode of, say, a Mickey Spillane for a Mike Hammer. Now sitting on a bench, eating what looked to be a sandwich while reading what looked to be a newspaper…

"Yo, Mr. Maximo," said the not so usually sharp-eyed trainee he had taken under his wing. "What's up with the disguise?"

"Working an undercover lay involving that 'Herstory' teacher, the Phlegming broad, and…"

"Oh yeah? Ms. Phlegming's got my tighty-whities in a bunch too," said the kid. "Have a seat and help yourself to one of my spare sandwiches."

Hmmm.

He was feeling peckish, and seeing as how the offer was for what looked to be ham-on-rye, one of his favorites… Max temporarily ditched the disguise and plopped his own oversized backside onto the bench.

"Members of the Intersectionals Club—kids who identify as victims of multiple intersecting marginalizations mainly related to gender, sexual preference, race and species—are planning to go on strike and demonstrate for what they think would be social justice for others and themselves," the kid explained. "Ms. Phlegming is the club's faculty advisor, and gave everyone in Herstory class an option to either demonstrate solidarity for her assigned causes or write a twenty-page paper about a *Mayflies Manifesto* published back in the day by an old guy named Professor Lehough, who lived right here in town and led a protest against a golf tournament."

Yeah, Max remembered Lehough from past run-ins with the

oddball, and after being reminded by the kid—who had opted to write a twenty-page paper—he recalled in detail that ten years ago the town had put on a bigtime golf tournament that went sideways. Sponsored by a federal government Program for Inter-Generational Sports, the idea of the P.I.G.S. event was to reduce if not eliminate the threat to national security posed by friction between Americans of different generations.

According to ex-President Obama, encouragement of people of all ages to let off steam by playing together like children would lead to a fairer, kinder, more gentle society of young, middle-aged, and old. But the tournament was a flop, in part because…

"Professor Lehough led the protest by Boy and Girl Scouts," said the kid, "because he thought the P.I.G.S. Program was a Democrat Party attempt to gloss over what he called the biggest theft of wealth in history."

Heist of wealth?

Max recalled that the Mayor, Booster Bailey, had almost bankrupted the town by putting out bonds to build the Hogback Hot Links golf course for the tournament. The kid now further reminded him the professor and Scouts got up in arms against the Baby Boomer generation for getting old, staying healthy and well-off while kids' health declined and youthful poverty increased. Lehough blamed the government making unfair "transfer payments" from young to old in the form of Social Security and Medicare funding.

"Ms. Phlegming put a picture of the professor on her classroom wall, next to another new one of Mao Somebody, who led a Cultural Revolution in China back in the 1960s and 70s. And like I say, she's made us non-protesters write essays about the *Mayflies Manifesto* that got published when the town had a newspaper called *The Weekly Herald*."

Max also recalled that the town's golf course got closed down and the bonds paid off by the federal government when Lehough made a stink about the hogback west of town being a habitat for an endangered breed of insects.

"According to the professor, there is much about social

sciences to learn from study of natural sciences," the kid continued, "including in particular study of mayflies. Specifically, Professor Lehough noticed that unlike Baby Boomers—living longer than prior generations and hogging bigger slices of American pie—mayflies exist in larva form for a carefree period comparable to human childhood, blossom into 'puberty' to mate, and die that very day or the next, content to have 'lived large' and fulfilled their purpose in life."

Free Luigi!…Stand up for youth in Asia!…Take down Tesla!…

What in Sam Hill?

"The Intersectionals Club protest must have started in the Free Speech Zone around the corner," the kid explained. "Ms. Phlegming told them to try to keep it mostly peaceful, but by the sounds of it…"

Save democracy!…Cancel election of Trump!…Save youth in Asia!…

Hmmm.

Max could see how high school Intersectionals and the Phlegming broad—no doubt watchers of CNN News—would be het-up against Trump occupying the White House, but was surprised and puzzled that they would have such a case of red-ass about electric cars, not to mention…

"What are you two boys up to?" said Roberta, suddenly standing over them. "Just 'hanging out' as usual, telling tales about imagined 'luck' with girls?"

"Just, uh, helping the kid with his homework. He's a protege of sorts and…"

Save democracy!…Save Hamas!…Save Youth in Asia!…

"You should be participating in these shenanigans with other, uh…Mindless protest by adolescents is a traditional right of passage, part of growing up," said his other protege of sorts, nodding in the direction of the high school student ruckus, and sounding more like his mother than his sounding board.

"Yours Truly is all for free speech, and democracy," said Max. "But currently focused on…What are you up to, Roberta? You

should be taking a nap before your hospital shift."

"Came by to have a chat with Claudette Phlegming. Understanding what must be the frustrations involved in taking care of our client, I'm sure I will wrap up the 'case" while you sit here, eating sandwiches and gaining more weight."

Max bit his tongue, suspicious that his would-be "partner" might be a little too "understanding" of the Phlegming broad's "frustrations".

Support youth in Asia!…Fight for youth in Asia!…Direct action now!…

CHAPTER FOUR

♫ *Trying to please two women is like a ball and chain/ Sometimes the pleasure ain't worth the strain . . .* ♫

Seated at his high school Principal's desk… humming beneath his breath to the tune of an old country-and-western song… Howard Taylor signed a personal check for deposit into a Mr. & Mrs. saving account, then inked its amount into a ledger:

$200.00

He did the simple math and came up with the current account balance:

$2,200,00

He hurled his fountain pen against a wall, then mentally noted the approximate cost of the fancy check-writing instrument—a Christmas present—indirectly paid for out of his own pocket:

$200.00

♫ *When you try to please two women, you can't please yourself/ At best it's only half good; a man can't stock two shelves…* ♫

Recent dental work for the Missus had made a serious dent in their so-called rainy day fund, already depleted by his trip to Plymouth Rock last Thanksgiving for a teachers conference. Not a week passed without financial "precipitation" if not "hail". And even abnormal cloudless days were expensive.

Darn it, he was already past the early retirement he had looked forward to. At age fifty-three, he was still babysitting teenaged brats for meager pay, and at the end of the tunnel the teachers pension program was underfunded. That he might be recognized—if only for longevity—as State, or even County Principal of the Year, would possibly bring with it a bonus and

pay boost, but…

♪*It's a long old grind, and it tires your mind…* ♪

Howard sighed. He'd given up bowling, his prior once-a-week recreational activity. He'd cancelled twice-a-month barber shop maintenance of his once-prized flat-top, and now shaved his head. He himself had not had even a routine dental exam and cleaning for three years. Bottom line: he could not afford to remain married to a recovering gum disease victim and also keep…

He had not thought of Claudette as a "mistress" following the faculty Christmas party almost two years ago. He had thought of her as still his subordinate at work and occasional off-duty sex partner until her birthday came 'round and she more or less demanded a remembrance in the form of jewelry. For following occasions calling for *Hallmark Cards*, including his own birthday, she had asked for envelopes stuffed with cash. Still, he had not thought of her as even potentially a second wife until…

Darn it, Claudette's aged mother had moved in with her. The crotchety old biddy's constant physical presence had not only interrupted his sole remaining "recreational activity", it had also added to his "responsibilities". Claudette had promised to, uh, "get rid of" the financial burden of housing her mother, but had failed to…

"Sorry to interrupt, Mr. Taylor," said his administrative assistant, Bertha Botsford, rushing into his office. "Intersectionals got past the Dobermans into the Free Speech Zone and need to be put down ASAP!"

Howard dashed from his office…down a hallway…and into an open courtyard.

Fight for youth in Asia!…Fight for Palestinians!…Jews out of China!…Jews out of Palestine!…

Darn it, he had once boasted that Henryetta High School under his command had become the Harvard of Okmulgee County, and sure enough…

Stand with Luigi!…Stand with youth in Asia!…Stand with Palestinians!…

As Principal of HHS, nominally in charge of buildings, grounds, students and…

From the river to the sea!…Youth in Asia must be free!… Free Luigi!…Free Teslas for all!…

Aha! Off to one side, calmly watching the dangerous spectacle in progress was his…was a member of the faculty, and no doubt the instigator of the student demonstration in support of not only Palestinians, but now…He rushed to the rabble-rouser's side.

"Darn it, Claudette, as Principal of the 'Harvard' of Okmulgee County I publicly stated that we, like the other Harvard, will stick to our core mission and no longer voice positions on controversial political issues. As a faculty member under my command, you…"

"I'm not 'voicing' anything, Howard. And do not ever again refer of me as 'under' you," said his recreational sex partner, a radical feminist, though not a dog lover, who had refused to assume the so-called missionary position on grounds that it was demeaning to women. "The students are spontaneously exercising their right to freedom of speech in the Zone."

Fight for youth in Asia!…Fight for Palestinian martyrs!… Fight for democracy!…

"You saw what happened to that Principal of Harvard who tolerated what was then controversial antisemitic 'free speech' on campus after strictly condemning 'triggers'—such as the word 'field'—that hurt the feelings of Black students and those otherwise demeaned as cotton pickers."

Solidarity with Palestinians!…Solidarity with youth in Asia!…Solidarity with solidarity!…

"What I saw was that my namesake—Dr. Claudette Gay—got out of her onerous administrative duties amid accusations of petty plagiarism, and returned to her tenured position as a professor teaching a single class at a salary of one million dollars a year!"

"HHS is not actually a 'Harvard', Claudette. We don't have endowments from foreign countries for teaching positions. We don't even have money for…"

"Money, money, money! Unlike Dr. Gay—yes, also a woman, but luckily Black—I myself was cut off from loans for continued graduate education that would have earned me a PhD and tenured employment at the actual Harvard."

Claudette had borrowed and spent over four hundred thousand dollars for more than ten years of matriculation at various graduate schools, from which she had earned four Masters Degrees in what? Nothing but…

Youth in Asia will be free!…From the river to the sea!… Everything will be free!…From the River to the Sea!…

"'Not for nothing did I earn a Masters in Herstory from Wellesley! 'Not for nothing did I get not only a Masters in LGBT Studies from NYU but also a third graduate degree in Self Esteem from Fresno State University! And a fourth one in Marxist Tactics for Destruction of Western Civilization via Ti Tok from Chow Ching University, the Harvard of Hunan Province!"

Free Palestinians!…Free Youth in Asia!…Free health insurance!…Free lunch!…

With his continued employment and pension going up in smoke, Howard conceded that antisemitic chants were no longer deemed controversial by academics, and that support for the killer of an insurance company executive was justified, but…but, darmnit, what was up with this new line of forest fire in support of…?

Youth in Asia!…Youth in Asia!…Youth in Asia!…

"Just mindless sounds, Howard, like Mao's slogans during the great Chinese Cultural Revolution. 'Eat the Rich', for example. One can't expect teenagers to understand what words mean. Like rap so-called music, not until sounds of words rhyme—'Palestine free' and 'river to sea', for instance—do they become even half-baked ideas in the befuddled minds of American youth."

"Then what's the point of allowing them, even encouraging them to mindlessly chant? If the State Department of Education gets wind of this…this 'free speech', my pension…"

Stand for youth in Asia!…March for youth in Asia!…Fight

for youth in Asia!…

"The point of student protest is that progressive media will magnify the imagery and translate the sounds. Politicians and this current generation of so-called 'helicopter parents' will think the little darlings have something to say," said the holder of a Master's Degree in Marxist Tactics.

"But to what end, Claudette? Jews are not occupying China and slaughtering uninsured Asian youth."

"The objective is to launch an American cultural revolution like Mao did in China, and…"

Mao! OMG! Howard saw his chances of being named even a semi-finalist for even County Principal of the Year reduced to ashes.

"…and shake up the corrupt American capitalistic system, damnit. To the Chairman's slogan of 'Smash the Four Olds'—old ideas, old customs, old culture and old habits—the time has come to smash old people."

Jews out of Palestine!…Youth in Asia in Palestine!…Jews out of Asia!…

"Criminy, Claudette, those teenagers in China's so-called cultural revolution became bloodthirsty Red Guards. They actually resorted to cannibalism, but with appetites mainly for underpaid school administrators, teachers and other intellectual elites."

"Damnit, Howard, not until this corrupt capitalist country gets bloodsucking oldsters off the tit will the American federal government have no excuse to not cancel my student debt."

Ha! Claudette was a career-student whose loans were not costing her anything out of pocket. She was not paying and had not paid a dime on her outstanding debt, but…

"Until I am deemed 'credit worthy' by those bloodsucking capitalist bankers, fascist politicians won't give me a new loan to pursue a PhD. In the meantime, Howard…"

Claudette jerked her head sideways and directed a stink-eye toward…Uh oh, in a ridiculously transparent "disguise" the fat man who had been dogging her was standing off to the side of

the student demonstration.

Most recently, the nosy Notary Public had accused Claudette of spiking cafeteria food with overdoses of soybeans — supposedly natural suppressors of testosterone — in order to weaken boy wrestlers and make her girls badminton team look better by comparison. The charge had blemished Claudette's reputation and, in her view, ruined her chances of getting the badminton chair on the faculty of the real Harvard. She was already on probation and…

"He knows too much about the, uh, background of a certain real estate transaction," said Claudette. "Your job, Howard, is to, uh, take care of the fatso," his, uh, partner hissed. "You owe me that for what all that I'm doing for you."

Damnit, only now did Howard fully understand — and empathize with — remorseful rats caught in traps, driven to chew off their own testicles to escape the consequences of their appetites.

From the river to the sea!…Youth in Asia must be free!… From the river to the sea!…Luigi must be free!

CHAPTER FIVE

At the kitchen table inside the house he had shared with his mom since birth, Max worked on a slice of beef brisket while also chewing, so to speak, on gristle, again so to speak, embedded in *Case of Broad With an Itch*.

Staking out today's high school scene, he'd confirmed by personal eyeball that the Phlegming broad and the high school Principal were tight as two feet in a wet boot, but…Dang it, despite his disguise, the cozy couple had made him. Yours Truly's investigation into their plot was at a dangerous standstill.

"Max, first let me say that I think it is highly unlikely that Claudette Phlegming ever attempted to kill her mother by putting a pillow over her face," said Mom. "For one thing, matricide is rare, and almost never committed by daughters."

"Exactly. That's why the broad thought she herself could do the dastardly deed for her cohort, and get away with it. Less likely than a third party doing the old lady would be suspicion of a daughter committing mother murrrderrr in a devilishly clever switcheroo of the plot in *Case of Throw Momma From the Train*."

"For another thing, poor old Minnie Phlegming—bless her heart—has, well, I hate to say it," said Mom, "but at recent Bible study meetings she has appeared to be, perhaps, a bit tipsy. And Minnie has always been inclined to speak somewhat unkindly about her oldest daughter for failing to be attentive."

"Which makes it more incriminating in Yours Truly's book that the 'inattentive' daughter would move the old lady into her house for personal TLC."

"So let me get this theory of yours straight," said Mom,

carving another slice of brisket for him. "You think matricide was attempted by Claudette Phlegming at the behest of Mr. Taylor, in return for which the high school Principal is to bump off you, putting neither under suspicion for the murder each wants committed."

Yeah, that was the twisted plot in a nutshell.

"I can see why Claudette Phlegming would be, uh, upset with you," Mom continued. "The two of you have been at sixes-and-sevens for years. But otherwise, no, your so-called case has nothing in common with that old 'documentary film' except for an alleged threat against an elderly 'momma'."

Nothing in common?

Max had made a mental list of matching factors, including, for instance, that the momma threatened with getting thrown from a train was reportedly "paranoid" that her son was plotting to put her away in an old folks home. And in Yours Truly's earlier case, the document that the Phlegming broad had wanted him to stamp was a deed for sale of her mother's house.

"Well, yes," said Mom, "it's common for we 'seniors', especially women, to worry about being dumped into retirement quarters, but still… Why would Mr. Taylor want to have Claudette rub out her mother?"

Yeah, that was a bit of gristle alright.

On the other hand, Old Lady Phlegming might have got wise to, and might have disapproved of her daughter's relationship with Taylor. The high school Principal might have his nose out of joint and/or see the old lady as….

"Well, yes, if what you say is right, which I doubt, why wouldn't Minnie disapprove of her daughter's behavior, and Howard Taylor's too! He is a married man, for heaven's sake."

Hmmm.

Mom was always at least half right. And if the Principal was happily married…

Hmmm.

Maybe the Phegming broad was not in cahoots with Taylor, and didn't expect the high school Principal to scratch her back

by offing Yours Truly.

Hmmm.

And/or maybe Mom was right that Old Lady Phlegming had got it wrong about someone trying to snuff her.

Yeah, the elderly broad had copped to fluttering chest pains and a bladder release, but admitted she had glimpsed only a pillow—not bright white light—before seeing "blackness". And in *Case of Throw Momma From the Train*, the momma complained of having only a nightmare of being murrrderrred by a Black trumpet player named Louis Armstrong!

Hmmm.

"What does Roberta have to say about your suspicions?" said Mom. "Daughters and mothers often get sideways with one another, and in fact, Roberta's mother—may she rest in peace—was continually fussing with Roberta's sister. My advice is that you butt out and let your, uh, helpmate handle the 'case'."

Dang it, prior to his discovery of Brad Runyon a/k/a the original Fat Man as his role model, his mom—obviously disappointed that he'd not turned out to be a girl—had encouraged him to think of himself as Jessica Fletcher of *Murder, She Wrote* fame. And now his so-called "helpmate"seemed to have become practically a daughter to her. But...

Roberta, yeah, she'd read a lot of pulp case reports and watched a lot of documentary films, but when it came to doping out what was cooking in a current, not already documented case...Come to think of it, his mom's encouragement of Roberta Peters keeping company on a different sofa might have had less to do with his alleged need for privacy, and more to do with her wanting Roberta to "butt out" of her kitchen. Too many cooks spoiled broth and...

With his theory of the case now looking to be possibly half-baked, so to speak, Max now realized that his prior sofa mate had got in the way of Yours Truly himself unravelling a possibly single plot by only Claudette Phlegming to cook only her mother's goose, again so to speak.

In a way, what a relief! Yours Truly might not be in danger of getting bumped off, but…In another way, dang it, Roberta would get credit for "wrapping up" *Case of a Broad With an Itch*!

WEDNESDAY

October 15, 2025

CHAPTER SIX

Max drove the brown boiler toward the local hospital.

Last night in bed, the more he had second-guessed his second theory of *Case of a Broad With an Itch*, the more he'd come to doubt that a daughter—even Claudette Phlegming—would attempt to personally bump off the elderly woman who had stumbled into his office. But this morning…

"And tell her I'm out of gin, again!" Old Lady Phlegming had shouted through the blower…after ranting about mistreatment at the hands of her oldest daughter…complaining at length about a wax ball in her ear…and again claiming that she had been the intended victim of matricide, witnessed by her other daughter, Penny.

Now, arrived at the hospital's Emergency entrance, Max could see how either or both Phlegming sisters—not to mention a casual acquaintance or random passerby—would want to put a pillow on the cranky old woman's face.

"Were you dropped off for emergency medical attention?" said a dame behind a hospital counter.

"Fit as a fiddle. Here to see a nurse named Penny about an urgent private matter."

"Penny's on duty in the Intensive Care Unit, down the hallway and to the right."

Ankling into the ICU, a dimly lit room…quiet as a tomb except for bleeps of machines hooked up by wires and hoses to patients… all lying still as corpses in a row of beds…

"Hey, Sunshine, got anything to brighten the day of this poor woman over here?" said a guy, who—decked out in one of

those light green scrubbing outfits — looked to be a doctor. Max reached into a pants pocket for coins, but…

"Money won't put a smile on her face, not after yesterday's botched amputation of a leg. This little lady needs to be told a joke."

A joke? Max couldn't immediately come up with a funny punch line appropriate for the circumstances.

"Saving 'em all for younger and hotter chicks, huh? Can't spare a little mirth for an old and ugly one in need of being put in stitches."

Hmmm.

"Okay, a joker ankled into a bar and met a one-legged dame named Eilene."

Crickets.

"She worked at IHOP."

"Fine, keep your good material for lookers. Have babes in bars rolling in aisles. Make 'em laugh their pants off."

A Knock Knock joke came to mind, but before he could knock…

"Carry on with your chores, Kenny," said a female voice, and… As the guy ankled away, Max noticed that he had a mop in hand.

"Kenny thinks all doctors are quacks, and that laughter is the best medicine," said a dame also decked out in light green scrubs, identified by nameplate as a "Penny".

Max introduced himself and — allowing the dame's mistaken impression that he was from the County Human Services Department to go uncorrected — proceeded to grill the Phlegming broad's semi-lookalike sister about their mother's claim of attempted matricide.

"Wel-l-l-l, uh, yes," said the now obviously nervous nurse. "During an emergency delivery of, uh, medicine, I did walk in as Claudette was, uh, fluffing Mom's pillow, but…Our aged mother — she's sixty-five — often has nightmares about being assaulted by…"

"Let me guess. A Black trumpet player named Louis Armstrong, right?"

"No, her nightmares are about being sexually assaulted by President Trump. Mom worries about…Well, since selling her house to pay-off Claudette's delinquent mortgage and moving in with her, even my husband and I have to help with rent and, uh, medicine not covered by Medicare. If she loses her Social Security…"

Hmmm.

"It's only natural for Mom to get crankier as she ages. Even though her cot is next to a furnace—my sister uses her spare bedroom for yoga—it gets cold down there in that damp, windowless basement."

Hmmm.

"So of course my sister gets, uh, exasperated at times, when caring for Mom interferes with her other activities. But attempted 'matricide'? No, Claudette would not have resorted to such a drastic measure."

His revised theory of *Case of A Broad With An Itch* looked to have also been off the mark, but then…

"So-called 'granny dumping'—mainly for weekends and holidays—is not unusual for busy loved ones of old people," said the sister. "In fact, Claudette volunteers to make deliveries for others in our boat. Hospitals are required by law to admit them. And yes, many are left to face lonely deaths, and many bodies go unclaimed. But…"

Deliveries to death by boat?!

"…luckily, I myself happened to be on duty when Mom was found on a gurney in an Emergency Ward hallway. Claudette was off to another out-of-town seminar—one about Pilgrim Persecution of Pequods, as I recall—and I myself had a turkey in the oven at home. The seven days it took to officially identify the patient and do the paperwork…Well, a break from breathing those noxious furnace fumes in that damp basement was just what a doctor would have ordered for Mom if Medicare had allowed it."

Hmmm.

As his brain—like a hamster—spun a wheel inside his

head, Max recalled that discussing Hercule Poirot's *Case of the A.B.C. Murders*—yeah, murrrderrr in plural—was how and when Roberta and he had hit it off after being introduced to one another at her mother's funeral.

"I've already told all this to another Emergency Ward nurse who went through a similar experience with her mom," said the Phlegming sister. "She's now a part-time private investigator and said…"

Dang it, Roberta didn't have a P.I. license!

"…that she empathized with Claudette and would get in touch with my sister, to help her deal with the .. the problem of taking care of our mother."

Hmmm.

Percy Wilson's *Case of Killing With Kindness* came to mind, one of numerous reported cases of serial murders committed by hospital and nursing home "care givers", half of them dames using womanly means of insulin injection or suffocation. Before nailed, some had gotten away with snuffing dozens or even hundreds of patients in cases that were not investigated because victims were usually old if not sick. And no doubt others had gone—and were going—undetected.

If Old Lady Phlegming went toes-up…

Concerned that Yours Truly might be called onto a carpet for neglect of duty to report suspicion of elder abuse, Max mentally noted for the record that, yeah, he and Roberta Peters had talked, just talked about, uh, common interest in dickwork, but were never a Tommy-and-Tuppence Beresford husband-and-wife team. He had never authorized his, uh, acquaintance to undertake an unlicensed private investigation, and…

For the very reason that he'd had prior run-ins with Claudette Phlegming, Yours Truly himself would never have "empathized" with the broad about anything whatsoever, including but not limited to helping her deal with "the problem of taking care of" her mother!

Yeah, like every private dick from Hoboken, New Jersey to Henryetta, Oklahoma before him—Sam Spade to Phillip

Marlowe to Mike Hammer, and no doubt even Brad Runyon, the original Fat Man— Yours Truly may have been duped by a *femme fatale* posing as…as Hercule Poirot's unhelpfull sounding board, an Arthur Hastings.

CHAPTER SEVEN

Claudette stood at a kitchen window of her now debt-free bungalow, watching for arrival of her unreliable would-be "partner in crime". They had not had a daytime tryst for weeks, which was only one—and the least—of the many annoyances of having her chronically disapproving mother in residence. Ha! If the selfish old biddy only knew: she would not be living her so-called Golden Years in comfort—likely would not be living at all—but for the contributions toward the costs of her welfare wheedled from Howard.

Not to mention the many other sacrifices of a dutiful daughter. But gratitude? Her mother, Minnie, didn't know the meaning of the word. Like other coddled members of the current geriatric generation, her mother insisted she was entitled to be paid back money "put away" by her late spouse and herself. In fact, it was money currently being paid into the government's Social Security racket by younger generations that kept a doomed boatload of old people frown sinking.

Ebenezer Scrooge got a bum rap. When told by a do-gooder that the poor would rather die than be put in debtors prison, Scrooge advised them to go ahead and die, to reduce the surplus population. In today's world, however, old people were not poor. Kept in comfort, they kept on selfishly living.

Claudette ground her teeth. Pension funds together with government payments heisted from hard working, underpaid, tax-paying school teachers such as herself had been designed to keep the current crew of ancient mariners afloat for their timely docking on the shores of the River Styxx, so to speak. But no,

though overcrowded and leaky, the warm tub of butter occupied by 69 million so-called Baby Boomers—holding on for dear life to 54% of the nation's wealth—continued to stubbornly bob offshore.

The financial burden imposed on currently middle-aged people by the younger so-called "Boomerang Generation"—that she herself was blessedly free of—was a pittance compared to having a free-loading old "Boomer" move in, and no doubt less disruptive to…

At the sight of Howard clumsily trying to clamber over a backyard fence, Claudette—to mask sounds of his clandestine visit—turned on a radio that sat on a window sill. Fittingly enough, an Oldies song…

♫**She works hard for the money/ So hard for it, honey…** ♫

Though nine years older than her, Howard was also one of 72 million members of Generation X, owners of only 26% of country's money, and the first American generation destined to end up worse off than parents, many with no savings for retirement versus almost $300,000 socked away by the average Boomer. But unlike her vocational "superior", she had not been born with a penis and…

♫**She works hard for the money/ She works hard for the money…** ♫

"Shhh!" Claudette shushed after opening the backdoor for her discreet bag man. "My mother has ears like an elephant."

"What the heck, Ms. Phlegming, you walked out in the middle of a class," Howard whispered. "And leaving that graphic message with my assistant was indiscreet."

♫**She works hard for the money/ So you better treat her right…** ♫

"I myself got an obscene call from my sister," she hissed. "That fat man you were supposed to take care of tracked down Penny at the hospital, asking questions about how I, uh, we have been treating Minnie and…"

"Treating her like a queen, I would say. And before you ask, my outlays for your mother's upkeep have passed the point that…"

"Who's that up there with you, Claudette?" said guess who through the intercom that she, or technically Howard, had paid for, along with a dumbwaiter to make onerous trips downstairs almost unnecessary. **"What is this, a cat house!"**

Claudette turned off the radio and turned on the intercom's basement speaker.

"Just, uh, the mailman, Minnie. Turn up the tv for your shows."

"Better not let that sugar daddy of yours catch you *en flagrante*. He's dumb, but not completely stupid."

"Pay no attention, Howard," she whispered. "She's old, and senile."

"As I was about to say, uh, Claudette. I now realize that I cannot afford to keep…"

"And as I was about to more importantly say, Howard, that fat man is also a private detective! When I dropped Minnie off yesterday to wander around for a while in downtown traffic, she must have stumbled into his cubicle and made my, uh, our cause sound, uh, criminal!"

"Which cause? Cancellation of your student debt? Reparations for lost income resulting from denial of your right to a PhD? Death to Jewish bankers, and dentists? Support for Palestinian martyrs and youth in…?"

"The cause for solving all my, uh, our problems, Howard. My self-centered mother must be taking it personally, and must have told that fat man…"

"Give that horny high school Principal what he wants and get down here, Claudette!"

"As we both know, I'm the brains, you're the muscle, Howard. Your job is to take care of…"

"My muscle is worn out, Claudie," said "Howie", an understatement, to put it kindly. "Weighing the risk of getting gum disease against the costs of continuing…"

"I can't hear my shows with this earwax ball."

"How dare you compare our relationship to your wife's disgusting periodontal issues!"

"I'm sorry, Ms. Phlegming: I simply cannot afford to keep a

mistress and, uh, an illicit 'mother-in-law'… or divorce my wife."

As Howard-the Coward turned on a heel and retreated through the back door…

"Damnit, I changed your diapers, Claudette. A daughter's duty to her mother is to come down here and scratch my back in return!"

Claudette turned on the radio…

♫**A common cold will fool ya/ And whooping cough can cool ya/ But poison ivy, Lord, will make ya itch…** ♫

… and went to the stairway leading to the basement.

♫**She's pretty as a daisy/ But look out for her, she's crazy/ She'll really do you in/ If you let her get under your skin…** ♫

Ding. Dong.

At the front door, "Sorry to bother you at home, Claudette," said a homely middle-aged woman wearing green hospital scrubs. "You were otherwise engaged at the high school yesterday, and I just want you to know that when it comes to putting up with an aged cranky mother, well, Ive been there and done that. You are not alone. I understand and empathize. If I can be of any help…"

♫**…while you're sleepin'/ Poison ivy comes a creepin' around** ♫

CHAPTER EIGHT

Max parked the brown boiler at the Main Street curb out front of Mister Quickie's and ankled into the copy shop to pick up his Roscoe. The exact replica of Mike Hammer's "Old Junior" did not actually squirt lead, but packing the fake heat for his grilling of the Phlegming broad's sister would have set off alarms. Doctors and staff were known to be tetchy about outsiders also carrying lethal weapons on hospital premises. Relatives of patients, het-up about medical bills…

"Yo, Mr. Max," said the kid, seated in the client chair, snacking on a muffin no doubt dispensed by the on-site vending machine Quickie had installed in the workstation cubicle as a perk for copy shop customers. "Any chance you could use some, uh, additional help doping out *Case of A Broad With an Itch*, or need someone to start jotting a case report?"

In a hurry, but peckish, Max—also firm in the belief that a man stood tallest when stooping to help a kid—plopped himself into his double-wide chair, accepted the offer of a spare muffin, and decided to put the young case report jotter wise to the updated status of his current lay.

"The perp in *Case of Throw Momma From a Train* got cold feet and rescued his momma from being chucked out the rear of a caboose by a cohort," he began, "but later in the documentary claimed the old lady died of, quote: 'old age'."

"So, what's the point?" said the kid, with pencil poised to jot in a small notebook.

"The point is that at our local hospital, the Phlegming broad has been dumping old ladies by the boatload," Max explained.

"Yeah, I can see how you might think that's odd," said the young jotter, looking up from the notebook with an unshocked look on his kisser. "Ms. Phlegming talks all the time about people over sixty-five lolling in hospitals and coming out pale but alive and well rested. With expensive new hips, new knees, and even new vital organs that extend their unnatural lives and siphon off…"

"It's all part of a smokescreen, kid, to hide her real plot. But Yours Truly saw through the haze and…"

"But she must have a soft spot when rhetoric meets reality," said the young wannabe, obviously overboard in water way over his head. "Members of the Intersections Club who have driver's licenses—'Charon's Ferry Squad', Ms. Phlegming calls them—are voluntold to pick up oldsters and take them to the hospital for treatments, and no doubt new organs in some cases."

"Treatments?! Wake up and smell the chloroform, kid. Phleming and the fairies have been planting crops for the Grim Reaper to finish off, sometimes right at the curb outside the hospital entrance."

Max explained that after the other Phlegming broad copped to her sister's personal "volunteer work", he had checked hospital records, and bingo. Multiple local grannies had bought farms recently.

"But Mr. Max, that's not proof of…"

"In other words, Yours Truly is now faced with another re-play of *Case of the A.B.C. Murders*."

"The grannies died in alphabetical order?" said the clueless kid.

"Forget the alphabet angle, Sherlock. The A and B in Poirot's case were red herrings, intended to throw Scotland Yard cops off the scent of what was really afoot."

Max patiently reminded his protege—still wet behind his stuck-out ears and slow on the uptake—that in *Case of the A. B. C. Murders*, rub-outs of A and B were to set up the whack-jobbing of a C—a certain Carmichael Clark, brother of a bromicidal joker named Franklin Clarke—to make Poirot and

the cops think a deranged serial killer was at work and deflect suspicion from what was really afoot.

"Yeah, I know," said the kid, rising from his chair. "But gee, Mr. Max, we've already applied Mr. Poirot's case to another lay. I hope you're not getting…not old and 'forgetful', but, uh, maybe stuck in a rut."

"No way, José," said Max. "Yours truly—not 'we'—is still sharp as a freshly ground Number 2 pencil. The Phlegming broad is plotting to hide matricide like a needle in a haystack of other dead grannies."

With no sign of a light bulb appearing above his head, so to speak, the kid put his pencil back behind a stuck-out ear, got up from his chair with a sigh, and ankled from the cubicle.

With a sigh of his own, Max retrieved his Roscoe from a desk drawer and got to his feet. He would have his mom make a sack of sandwiches and a thermos of coffee for a stake-out of the hospital's Emergency entrance. Sooner or later --tonight or another night—Yours Truly would nab the teenaged volunteers working for the Phlegming broad—maybe catch the ringleader herself—in the act of grand matricide a/k/a grannicide!

But then… as he hotfooted from the cubicle, it hit him like a knuckle sandwich to the chops: In addition to Claudette Phlegming's longstanding grudge against Yours Truly, by now Roberta Peters—"empathizing" with Phlegming and helping the matricidal daughter take care of "the problem of taking care" of her crotchety mother—had no doubt put the deadly dame wise that Yours Truly was onto her like dirty underwear. Realizing she was in a bind…

OMG, like another knuckle sandwich, it hit him: his own mom was an old person in danger of being picked up by teenaged vigilantes and—God forbid—dumped in a haystack!

CHAPTER NINE

With his desk tidied up and his personal affairs back in order, Howard leaned back in his office chair, closed his eyes, and contemplated a relatively rosy future.

♫*Easy Street/ No weekly payments you must meet…* ♫

Not that he didn't have ongoing concerns like everybody else. The wife's dental issues would continue to be financially onerous…their rainy day savings account was insufficient for weathering a downpour of other misfortunes…and by all accounts his pension, like that of other public service employees, was severely underfunded, but…

♫*Easy Street/ If I could live on Easy Street/ I'd want no job today…* ♫

He was overdue for a stroke of luck, and well deserved recognition. If he were to be named County or State Principal of the Year, a bonus and raise in salary…

Howard sighed, thankful that he had survived a typical male mid-life crisis without dire consequence. Now he was free of the "overhead" associated with his prior relationship with Claudette Phlegming. More importantly, ending of their "office romance" removed risk to his employment and pension, not to mention exposure to the costs of a divorce. He would miss being with his subordinate "privately", but would now have the time and wherewithal to get back to bowling and…

♫*Easy Street/ Nobody works on Easy Street/ They sit around and play…* ♫

Actually, he'd not had much "private recreational time" with Claudette for weeks, and had not much enjoyed their recently

few intimate moments together, due in large part to…

Bang!

Howard, startled, opened his eyes…jerked his torso upright and…Oh no, into his office came Claudette after slamming the door behind her.

"Howard, I have news that couldn't wait. My mother…Well, my sister must have over-supplied Minnie with gin. As I was trying to get her upstairs for a walk in the park and a breath of fresh air, she…Old people are inclined to fall and…

"Anyway, with the help of a nursing colleague of my sister who had happened to come by for a chat, I dropped her off at the hospital. Now we can have the love nest to ourselves."

Yeah, but —*ka-ching!* --the old woman's medical treatment would cost…

"I doubt Minnie will ever again be a financial problem, or otherwise a nuisance to us."

As Claudie came to him with "that look" in her eyes, Howard's resolve to do the sensible thing wavered, but…

"Sorry to interrupt, Mr. Taylor," said his administrative assistant, Bertha Botsford, barging into the office. "Two men from the State Department of Education are here, and say they have 'official business' that can't wait."

Official business? Such as announcement of a Principal of the Year award?

Two men dressed in gray business suits—one short and pudgy, the other tall and thin—marched into the office with briefcases in hand. Howard got to his feet and…

"This is, uh, Ms. Phlegming, one of our many Henryetta High School teachers I supervise, here to discuss, uh, the schedule for, uh, extracurricular activities," he felt compelled to explain. "She was just leaving."

"Ms. Claudette Phlegming?" said the tall, thin one, eyeing Claudette up-and-down. "Faculty sponsor of an 'Intersectionals Club'?"

"She'd better stay," said the short, pudgy one, glaring at Claudette. "This matter concerns the two of you."

The two of them? No way would Claudette be in line for recognition of any kind, except…

"We hardly know each other. Ms. Phlegming has worked here for only…"

"For more than two of my six long years in lower academia," said Claudette to the two men. "And I happen to be the faculty's union rep. What's that fascist Superintendent on the rag about now?"

Both representatives from Department headquarters in Oklahoma City declined his invitation to sit at a conference table, which Howard took to be a bad sign, not to mention their decline of his proffered handshakes and the scowls on their faces. As for his offer of refreshments…

"The Superintendent is 'on the rag' about almost everything having to do with our state's public education system," said the short, pudgy one.

"In particular, he is upset about yesterday's student demonstration here on the grounds of Henryetta High School," the tall, thin one explained.

"The protest against Trump's so-called election was spontaneous and mostly peaceful," said, uh, Ms. Phlegming. "Only few broken windows, a small fire, minor injuries to deserving redneck onlookers, and all confined to the school's Free Speech Zone. As Howard is wont to say: 'Henrietta High School is the Harvard of Okmulgee County'."

"Yes, for your past encouragement of antisemitic expressions of support for Palestinian martyrs, you are already on probation, Ms. Phlegming. And now…"

"I told her!" Howard exclaimed. "I warned Ms. Phlegming that her Intersectionals Club support for 'Youth in Asia' would lead to the teenaged malcontents becoming Red Guards murderously hungry enough to literally eat us alive. I myself am dead set against a Cultural Revolution that would do away with the four or five 'olds', including the Superintendent."

The two men gave him curious looks.

Claudette gave him a hard stink-eye.

"I knew teenagers would use new math and phonetic spelling against us," said Pudgy to his sidekick.

"I did not 'throw' my elderly mother back down the stairs!" Claudette blurted. "In addition to being old and feeble, she was intoxicated. Fell of her own free will, and is not dead yet."

"The Department condemns fear and loathing of old people in general."

"And your insidious incitement of organized 'Youth in Asia' is an unAmerican hate crime."

Howard's once rosy future, now gray and turning darker, passed before his eyes. He would lose his employment, and his pension. He would not be able to afford a return to bowling. And his wife's gums…

♫Beyond this mess ahead there is a street/ So very hard to find/ Though I have laid down my head/ At this dead end so many times/ Easy Street, on Easy Street… ♫

CHAPTER TEN

After again checking that front-door locks were secure, Max swiveled and again paced…After again checking that back-door locks were also set tight, he swiveled and again paced…Back at the front door, he re-checked, re-swiveled and…pacing past an open doorway to the kitchen…

"Max, for heaven's sake, sit down and have a bite of my pie," said Mom. "It's ridiculous of you to think Minnie Phlegming's daughter would try to vent hard feelings against you by 'bumping off' me."

Yeah, Mom had refused to go to a mattress, even after he'd put her wise to the connection between his *Case of A Broad With an Itch* and Hercule Poirot's *Case of the A.B.C. Murders.* By now her friend, Old Lady Phlegming, had probably been dumped like a needle in a haystack of bodies outside the hospital's Emergency entrance. In an Intensive Care Unit stall, it would likely be curtains for the Phlegming broad's mother within hours, if not minutes. And Roberta Peters would be on duty to help press a pillow against the old lady's face.

Max swiveled…he paced…he re-checked backdoor-locks…

Neither had his mom been personally alarmed by results of his online dickwork indicating that granny dumping was becoming common as fleas on old dogs since back in the 1990s, when a study of the craze uncovered that at least 70,000 elderly Americans had been abandoned in so-called care facilities during a single year. For crying out loud, almost two hundred hospital Emergency Departments reported that an average of eight grannies per week were dumped on their premises — more

during the Christmas holidays—some retrieved by family members or loved ones through police intervention, but most either abandoned or picked up by the Grim Reaper.

Obviously the Phlegming broad had joined a vast conspiracy to get rid of old moms, and Roberta…

Knock. Knock. Knock.

Max swiveled.

Knock. Knock. Knock.

Gingerly, he put his ear to the door, expecting to hear either the seductive voice of the Phlegming broad, luring him into the open, or the forked tongue of Roberta Peters, luring him onto a sofa. But…

"It's me, Mr. Maximo," he heard the kid's voice squeak. "I have news about Ms. Phlegming."

Max unlocked and opened the door.

"There's been a break in the case," the out-of-breath young case report jotter reported.

Max shut and re-locked the door.

"Oh hello, Mom Morgan. Is that the aroma of fresh baked apple pie I detect?"

Between mouthfuls of pie…his young protege spilled… that according to what his Uncle Ralph had heard from the high school Principal's assistant, Ms. Bertha Botsford… big cheeses from the State Department of Education had shown up that afternoon… and accused Phlegming of violating her probation for prior incitement of hate speech.

Between mouthfuls of another slice of pie, the kid went on to say that the Herstory teacher had previously made her class read a section of a book called *Gulliver's Travels*, in which a clan of foreign people called Struldburgs…after getting old…became opinionated, peevish, covetous, morose, vain and talkative… mainly about vices of younger people and deaths of the old… with no appreciation for anything except what they themselves had said and done during their own youthful and middle years.

"That doesn't sound like hate speech," said Mom, once a school teacher herself. "*Gulliver's Travels* used to be required reading."

"Yeah," said the kid, "but Ms. Phlegming ground her teeth and cussed out loud about how Struldburgs… by 'virtue' of nothing but old age… became proprietors of a whole nation that…because of their inability to properly manage… went to the dogs. She made Henry Rundell write a hundred times on the blackboard a quote from an old Roman man named Seneca the Younger: *Senecus mobidus est*, which means 'Old age is a disease'."

"Yeah, if the fuzz ever bust her, the Phlegming broad will no doubt use that line in court to justify dumping 'diseased' grannies at the hospital Emergency entrance," Max opined.

"That's only guesswork, not 'dickwork'," said Mom. "You don't know…"

"You were almost right, Mr. Max. According to Ms. Botsford via Uncle Ralph, yeah, Ms. Phlegming has been trying to get Intersectional Club members who have cars to take people to the hospital, though not necessarily to meet the Grim Reaper. She told the Department of Education investigators that the intended effect of the Association of American Against Retired People programs is to overload and bankrupt Medicare, leading Senators see to that it's both foolish and ultimately futile to keep old people unnaturally alive when the money could be better spent on, say, canceling student loans."

With the *Case of A Broad With an Itch* solved and the Phlegming broad exposed, Max eyed what was left of the apple pie. To make him fit enough for "marching", Roberta had put him on a diet, but now…

Knock. Knock. Knock.

Max went to the front door, again pressed an ear to it, and…

"Max, it's me, Roberta. I took off work when I heard the news about Claudette Phlegming."

"Yeah, with any luck your cohort might get what she deserves." Max answered through the door. "Same as you, Sweetheart, after they dig up your late mother's ashes."

"What on earth are you talking about?"

"The Phlegming broad's sister put me wise to you aiding-and-abetting the plot to commit matricide."

"Don't be ridiculous. As a daughter who also got stuck taking care of an elderly parent, I simply empathized with the Phlegming sisters who were similarly trapped."

"Yeah, sure, tell it to the judge."

"Damnit, to take care of my aging mother I gave up hopes of marriage and any other kind of romantic relationship. I had to settle for left-overs not fit to march down an aisle or perform other manly duties. And you—a mama's boy whose mother wants to get rid of—were at the bottom of the barrel."

Back in the kitchen, Max sat down at the table—explained that it was a misguided person at the wrong address who'd knocked—and dug into the apple pie.

"The main evidence that Ms. Phlegming and Mr. Taylor went too far by stirring up so-called 'direct action'…Well, I myself don't think the Intersectional Club members understood what Uncle Ralph called the 'subliminal phonetic message' hidden in what they were chanting for," the kid needlessly continued. "I think they were tricked by…"

"You mean those chants in support of 'Youth in Asia'? Yours Truly's got no beef with sending a few cans of food over to starving orphans in China."

"We used to do that good deed all the time," said Mom. "Encouraging teenagers to be charitable is not 'going too far' enough, in my opinion."

"'Youth in Asia' is approximately phonetic for e-u-t-h-a-n-a-s-i-a, Mom Morgan, as in senio-euthanasia, the merciful 'putting down' of elderly people such as yourself, like vets do to old dogs."

"Heavens to Betsy!" said Mom. "Who would take care of Max?"

THE
END